CW01501518

ACKNOWL⸱

I would like to thank all those who helped me with the development of this story.

Thanks to my very good friend Alison Lever for sharing her editing and technical skills. To Mark Richardson for reading an early draft, making useful suggestions and giving me the setting for the penultimate chapter, and to Andy and Maggie Wilkes for their continued enthusiasm and support.

I would especially like to thank my wife Anne for giving me some very useful insights and the whole family for putting up with me during the writing process.

Finally, my thanks to Paula Good and her team for turning my manuscript into the book you have before you.

It just remains to be said that all mistakes and errors are mine alone.

R L Mannings

PETER AND HANNAH

by

R.L. Mannings

British Library Cataloguing-In-Publication Data
A catalogue record of this book is available from the British Library.

ISBN 978-1-7394977-74

Cover Design by dartworks.design
Original Cover photo Alan James
Published via pgprintandofficeservices

Prologue

I knew what would happen when Hannah entered the room. Although she dressed to minimise the reaction of the men, it made little difference. By the early seventies, many women her age had adopted the mini-skirt and the media driven need to look 'sexy'. Her appearance seemed to be driven by a need to look drab. It didn't work.

She was quite tall. I knew she was around five foot eight because she seemed an inch or so taller than me. To ward off unwanted attention at parties, she would always head straight for me and put her arm through mine. She asked if I minded. Why would I?

Contents

PROLOGUE I

CHAPTER 1 1

CHAPTER 2 6

CHAPTER 3 13

CHAPTER 4 17

CHAPTER 5 24

CHAPTER 6 31

CHAPTER 7 41

CHAPTER 8 54

CHAPTER 9 76

CHAPTER 10 93

CHAPTER 11 103

CHAPTER 12 114

CHAPTER 13 125

CHAPTER 14 132

CHAPTER 15 153

CHAPTER 16 167

POSTSCRIPT 169

It's the 1970s and Peter, a young working-class lad, is unexpectedly asked out by an elegant young woman from a different social class. She makes clear he should have no romantic expectations, but says she needs his help. Peter accepts and, although they meet regularly, she reveals little about herself. She guards her secrets carefully, until by chance they begin to be revealed.

This is the story of two young people from different social worlds, the problems they face, and how they attempt to overcome them.

CHAPTER 1

I'd started to worry when I was young. When friends of my older sisters came to visit, they never seemed to notice me. They would talk about other friends and their relationships as if I wasn't there. I knew instinctively that any comment I made would not be received well. I developed a habit of staying quiet around girls. That was difficult, because I was always surrounded by them.

I can remember one friend asking me if I was a leg or a breast man. I thought he was talking about roast chicken and blushed when I was told he meant women. At that age, they were all obsessed with girls' bodies and how to get access to them. Why wasn't I? I certainly didn't like lads. In fact, I thought men were so ugly I had no idea what women saw in them. I knew little then of hormones and pheromones. An imbalance could have dangerous consequences. Maybe I lacked enough of both. Anyway, balls always drop in the end and mine were no exception.

One day, I asked my eldest sister why girls took no interest in me. She told me I had the features of a young boy, and girls are never interested in boys younger than themselves. I told Mum what Sally had said and she laughed and remarked that my boyish looks might be a disadvantage now but, in a few years' time, looking younger would be an advantage. My boyish appearance followed me through my teens. If there was a mystery, it was the mystery of why I didn't care.

*

Hannah was certainly a mystery to me. I was four years into my first job when I met her. I was working for a decorator who'd turned his hand to design. In the seventies, many better-off people were favouring modernism: straight lines, white walls and minimal clutter. Even if the houses they owned could be nothing other than Victorian, they insisted on covering spindled staircases with hardboard and throwing out highly decorated fireplaces. I thought it quite sad, throwing away history for the sake of a fad. I knew fashion went in cycles and what was being lost would be hard to recover.

It was in one of those houses that I met her. I wasn't quite sure where she fitted in and wasn't that curious. I was stripping off some ugly floss wallpaper when she passed me on the stairs. Without preamble, she asked me if I would accompany her to a party. I stared at her, but she didn't flinch. She was the most elegant person I'd come across. "Why ask the painter?" was my reply.

"Will you just do it? No strings and no romantic expectations, please."

No woman had ever asked me out, but I was bright enough to know the difference between 'accompany me' and 'take me'. From that moment on, I was one of the building blocks in the wall she was carefully constructing.

"Yes," I said. "So, what do I call you?" She looked at me through green eyes and curtains of long, black, shiny hair.

"Hannah," she said, and told me when and where I needed to be.

We met in the centre of town at the bus terminus. She looked me up and down as I approached.

"You'll do for tonight," she told me, "but next time – if there is one – I'll give you a few tips." I couldn't see anything wrong with my denims, white roll-neck sweater and casual jacket, but made no comment. She was dressed tastefully in a lightweight suit with flared trousers, so I thought her advice might be useful.

The party was in an area of town I wasn't familiar with. Tall Georgian houses with steps up to the front door. She led me to another set of steps which led down to the basement. The door was open and the place was already busy. If anybody lived in the house, it was clear they didn't live in the cellar. The room we entered was large and empty of furniture, but there were other, smaller rooms beyond it. Somebody had set up a record deck in one corner and a song called 'Stuck in the Middle With You' was blaring out through four large speakers. It was alright, but I had no idea who it was by. I thought some pop songs okay, but most had drivel for lyrics, where everyone was somebody's 'babe'.

Hannah dragged me through the dancers to what passed for a kitchen. Two old Belfast sinks were fixed to the wall with a large oak draining board between them. It was black in places where mould had gained a footing and whoever was charged with cleaning it had given up. On a rickety old table, which had been painted lime green, were two wooden barrels. One marked beer and the other cider. There were no glasses, just plastic things that looked like them. I stood by the wall near the entrance while Hannah fetched us two half pints of cider.

She stood next to me for a while, watching the others. It would have been impossible to talk in anything other than sign language as the music, and the people shouting over it, made meaningful conversation impossible. As neither of us could talk with our hands, silence was the only option. I didn't mind. It was interesting watching the reactions of the men who'd decided to approach Hannah. As soon as they got near, she would put her arm through mine and move close, as if she was about to whisper something in my ear. It was amusing to see their looks of disappointment.

"I think most of them have got the idea I'm with you, so I'm going to mingle on my own. There are lots of single girls here. Flirt if you must, but remember you're leaving with me." I wanted to ask her who the hell she thought she was, but I let it pass. To be honest, it was the first time I'd been the envy of other men, and I was quite enjoying it.

It's a strange thing that once one woman takes an interest in you, especially one like Hannah, then other women become curious. Almost as soon as Hannah had left my side, a petite blonde approached me. Her first sentence was a question. She asked how long I'd known Hannah. I replied that it had been a while and threw the question back to her. She didn't seem to know what to say and quickly changed the subject. She was at school with the host; it was her parents' house we were standing in. "It's very grand upstairs," she shouted at me, "and the parents don't mind her having parties when they're away. I would offer to take you up and show you around, but the door is always kept locked while the party is on." She invited me to meet her friends in one of the other rooms. I obliged, as it would save us from shouting into one another's ears. There was no way I was going to stand around waiting for Hannah's next call.

Hannah suggested that if anyone asked me what I did for a living I was to tell them I was in interior design and

PROLOGUE

I knew what would happen when Hannah entered the room. Although she dressed to minimise the reaction of the men, it made little difference. By the early seventies, many women her age had adopted the mini-skirt and the media driven need to look 'sexy'. Her appearance seemed to be driven by a need to look drab. It didn't work.

She was quite tall. I knew she was around five foot eight because she seemed an inch or so taller than me. To ward off unwanted attention at parties, she would always head straight for me and put her arm through mine. She asked if I minded. Why would I?

to try not to elaborate. As it turned out, this response produced no awkward questions. It seems that being 'in design' was acceptable, and in a way it was true. It was just that I was the guy who applied the paint rather the one who decided what the colour would be.

The blonde said her name was Natalie. She worked in admin for a local print company. The guys all seemed to have jobs that required them to wear suits: sales, office management, that sort of thing. I drifted away after a while and headed back to my place by the wall. It was quieter now. I think the host must have been instructed to keep the volume level down after ten. As soon as I arrived there, I could see Hannah heading toward me. A tall, thin guy was following close behind. She kissed me, put her arm around me, and stared at me with a doe-eyed expression. The guy faltered for a few seconds. Then he moved forward and held out a card. "If you ever need any financial advice, Hannah, do give me a ring." I took the card for her and gave the guy the nastiest look I could summon, while she continued to stare directly into my eyes. As soon as he'd gone she pulled away.

"You felt it, didn't you?"

"I felt something."

"I hate men like him. Whatever chemical he exudes is not going to bother me. Bastards like him are like those idiots who collect butterflies. They attract them to their net, stick their pin in them, add them to their collection, then forget all about them; bastards."

She turned back to me then, and asked if I would mind if we left.

CHAPTER 2

When I started work with him, he was known as John; now he insisted I call him Seth. He told me it was more like a designer's name than the name he'd been given. It did seem to suit him better, as he had a biblical look about him. He was a big man, with long black hair and a large thick, black beard streaked with white. He was less than ten years older than me, but had a lot of experience. I learnt a lot from him and his current wife Joyce. She was a fabric designer who'd left her husband for Seth after they'd met on one of Seth's projects.

Once the jobs were set up, Seth would use casuals or contractors for the prepping and base coats. I was the only full-time employee and would join him to do the finishing. He told me it was best that way. At the most important stage, the clients should feel they were getting our exclusive attention. Clients often became friends with Seth and Joyce.

One lunch break, Seth looked across at me. After staring at my face for a while he told me, "You wanna get rid of that bum fluff, boy. It makes you look even younger than people think you are."

This was the second time in a week I had been told to shave. On Sunday, my eldest sister Sally looked across the dinner table and laughed. "Is that hair on your upper lip, Pete? God, I know girls with more hair on their faces than you've got."

and sweaty, and just wanted to cool down. No chance of that. "Well, tell us?" Those were the words that came from the mouth of the youngest of my three older sisters as soon as I'd crossed the threshold.

"Tell you what?" I asked.

"Your posh girl rang and said she would ring back at six. Now, tell us all about her."

"Nothing to tell; she's just a friend," I said, as I hurried to the sanctuary of my half bedroom.

I never considered Hannah as posh, but when I thought about it I realised she had no trace of an accent. Caroline's comment made me realise that I knew nothing about Hannah, nothing at all. The sheer abundance of her presence seemed to forestall the asking of questions.

The closer it got to six, the more ambiguous I felt. I wasn't even sure if I wanted to answer the phone, but I knew someone else would and call me to it. Talking on a phone wired to the wall in a hallway where everyone could hear what you were saying was totally inhibiting. I was sure Caroline's ears would be twitching somewhere nearby. When the phone rang, I let her answer it. When she called up the stairs I made no effort to rush down them. I heard her say, "He's here," and when I got near she thrust the receiver into my hand. I didn't speak straight away, which forced Hannah into asking if I was there.

"Yup, what can I do for you?"

"I need a brother."

"You haven't got one?"

"No."

"Okay, but I need to know a bit more."

"I'll tell you on the night. Next Wednesday, if that's alright. Can we meet outside The Shakespeare. You know where that is, don't you?"

"No."

"By Redland Green. Try and get there before seven. For God's sake, Peter, don't leave me standing outside on my own."

"It's a long way from here. I'll do my best."

"You're cool."

"I don't think so."

Her laughter down the wires made me smile, but I still knew nothing about her.

I didn't need any more hints. On the way home from work, I called in to the chemist and made Mr Gillette a tiny bit richer.

Interior design was normally carried out in old period properties or large, very up-market, new ones.

Their owners were the only people who could afford Seth's prices. Because he was expensive, the work occasionally dried up. When it did, Seth was forced to take whatever work he could find. This was how I found myself on a small development of thirty houses working with the team of sub-contractors that Seth had organised. We were following the second fix carpenters from house to house. As soon as they finished hanging doors and fixing skirting, we moved in.

I didn't care for this sort of work. White doors and magnolia walls in endless succession. The team Seth had gathered were heads down, get-on-with-it types – apart from one, and there was always one. Cliff seemed to have it in for me. Most likely, because when Seth turned up and asked how the job was going it was always me that he asked. Cliff was the eldest on the team and had worked on and off for Seth for years. I guess he thought he should have been the one to be consulted first, rather than the upstart boy he considered me to be.

Being the target of three sisters who seemed to take it in turns to be irritable, I had developed a duck's back. Cliff had cottoned on to my boyish looks, and his comments about why I was wearing long trousers and not attending school just went unanswered. However, one lunch break his comments upset someone else on the team.

Most of the time you get the feeling when something's going to happen, but nobody did this time. We were at lunch in the dining room of one of the houses we were about to start painting. Most brought boxes of sandwiches. The joke was: what's today – ham, spam, or cheese? Mum always did her best, but it was usually one of these, with thinly sliced tomato when it was in season, and onion when it wasn't. We ate in silence until the flasks came out and we started pouring ourselves tea. Cliff suddenly burst out a question aimed at me. "Are you related to Seth? Or are you his little boy in some other way?"

He'd stood up to say these words and there was venom in his mouth when he said them. I just ignored him, but there was a big man called John who didn't. He came up behind Cliff, put his arms under Cliff's and clenched his hands around the back of his neck. Cliff couldn't move, and his face froze in fear.

John looked at me. "What do you want me to make this shit say, Peter? Apologise, ask forgiveness, or maybe we should take him and ask him to tell Seth what just came out of his mouth."

I knew Cliff had family and needed the money, so I wasn't about to get him sacked. For Christ's sake, he was just someone who Seth had favoured in the past and now some kid was being consulted instead of him. I told John to let him be. John told Cliff he was bloody lucky.

Later that day, John took me aside. "I fucking hate bullies; that bastard Cliff went too far." I nodded, and John proceeded to tell me a story.

"I was only fifteen and had been working on a big site in the city. Not painting then, but mixing mortar for a load of brickies. It was cold that winter, bloody cold. Most of my time was spent standing around between mixing new loads of mortar for the lads. That evening I complained to my sister about the cold and she told me to wear a pair of her old tights under my trousers. She was right: it took some of the edge off the cold. However, when I'd gone for a piss, one of the blokes had spotted them. Nothing was said, but at the end of the day four of them stripped my trousers from me, dumped me into a butt full of freezing cold water, then left me to find my way home. I know you don't need my help, Peter, but maybe that shit Cliff does."

Life is full of strange things; John and Cliff becoming friends was one of them.

Site work was boring, especially back then. Nowadays they try to vary the architecture a little. In the 1970s, housing estates were mostly full of identical boxes. Two-and-a-half-bedroom semis, Seth called them. I was brought up in one that my parents rented. Me in the half bedroom and my three sisters in one of the doubles. I tried to blank out the strife that went on between them, but I often heard things hitting the wall after a bout of screaming. Luckily, they were very protective of their 'little brother'. They still talk of me as being 'our little un'. They were infuriating, but I wouldn't have been without them.

We were a long way down the chain from the money, which meant that when something went wrong the first we'd hear about it would be to turn up and find the site gates closed. It was why everyone took their tools home at night. A firm goes tits-up and if your kit is on site, then nine times out of ten you can wave it bye-bye.

That morning, the gates were closed and there were some 'suit and ties' arguing with the site manager. A few minutes later the police turned up. They told us to go home and that we might be able to pick up any personal belongings later. None of us had left stuff on site, but Seth had some kit there. I was about to ask where the nearest phone box was when he drove up in the battered old Land Rover he thought did something for his image. His gift of the gab persuaded the suit and ties to let us on site to pick up the paint, brushes, and anything else he could legitimately claim as his. Turned out, Seth had paid our wages for the last week out of his own pocket. The cheque from the main contractors hadn't arrived. That was it. Next stop the dole office for John, Cliff and the others, but not for me; Seth had some news.

Joyce had come up trumps. She was visiting a client in Stoke Bishop. They were talking about a small chair upholstery job, when the woman said that what she would really like was someone to redesign the whole house. Joyce asked if she was serious; if she was, she would bring Seth along to talk to her. He knew his stuff and the woman was impressed. Six months or more of interesting work in a large mock Tudor house. No complaints from me, as I was beginning to see the world as one I had to paint entirely in contract Magnolia. Seth said that we might need a couple of extra hands; what did I think? He was surprised when I suggested Cliff and John.

Weekends were still weekends in the seventies. Sundays were still semi-sacred, with big shops closed and only small corner shops available for essentials. I liked it that way. The twenty-four/seven culture only ever benefits those who own the businesses; rarely those who have to work in them. I'm on God's side with this one.

*

It was a Sunday when I next heard from Hannah. I'd been out cycling with a friend. When I arrived home, I was hot and sweaty, and just wanted to cool down. No chance of that. "Well, tell us?" Those were the words that came from the mouth of the youngest of my three older sisters as soon as I'd crossed the threshold.

"Tell you what?" I asked.

"Your posh girl rang and said she would ring back at six. Now, tell us all about her."

"Nothing to tell; she's just a friend," I said, as I hurried to the sanctuary of my half bedroom.

I never considered Hannah as posh, but when I thought about it I realised she had no trace of an accent. Caroline's comment made me realise that I knew nothing about Hannah, nothing at all. The sheer abundance of her presence seemed to forestall the asking of questions.

The closer it got to six, the more ambiguous I felt. I wasn't even sure if I wanted to answer the phone, but I knew someone else would and call me to it. Talking on a phone wired to the wall in a hallway where everyone could hear what you were saying was totally inhibiting. I was sure Caroline's ears would be twitching somewhere nearby. When the phone rang, I let her answer it. When she called up the stairs I made no effort to rush down them. I heard her say, "He's here," and when I got near she thrust the receiver into my hand. I didn't speak straight away, which forced Hannah into asking if I was there.

"Yup, what can I do for you?"

"I need a brother."

"You haven't got one?"

"No."

"Okay, but I need to know a bit more."

"I'll tell you on the night. Next Wednesday, if that's alright. Can we meet outside The Shakespeare. You know where that is, don't you?"

"No."

"By Redland Green. Try and get there before seven. For God's sake, Peter, don't leave me standing outside on my own."

"It's a long way from here. I'll do my best."

"You're cool."

"I don't think so."

Her laughter down the wires made me smile, but I still knew nothing about her.

CHAPTER 3

Back when I was 14, puberty started to hit and I began to ask around. You couldn't find anything in the library that the librarians would let you have access to. Dad was useless; Mum gave me some clues. The whole process was described by the lads at school as your balls dropping. It doesn't come in one hit, so you have time to get used to it, but I still had a very slight high pitch to my voice. Balls dropping normally meant voice dropping. It wasn't so bad, but I was conscious of it.

The seventies was still an age where strict criteria was set for the label manhood. Most women used these criteria for judgement purposes, just like the men did. My boyish appearance often led other lads to ask, "Balls not dropped, then?" They definitely had, but I retained my appearance and they kept on asking until I escaped into the world of work. That was nearly four years ago and, apart from Cliff, nobody says anything. If they think me younger than I am they keep it to themselves

I managed to get to The Shakespeare a few minutes before Hannah arrived. That night there was a folkish look to her appearance. Before we moved, she turned and led me to the side of the building.

"Peter, I wanted to come tonight because two good musicians are playing here. However, there is a guy who turns up whenever they play and I can't shake him off."

We walked into the bar and Hannah led me to a large table which was surrounded by young men and women.

Then, they would have been called beatniks; now they're called hippies. At the other end of the bar was a group of folk musicians. One of the guys standing near them was staring at me and I stared back until he took his eyes away. That's the one, I thought. Tall, arrogant and self-important. Working with Seth in the houses of the rich, I'd come across his type before. The privileged boy forgetting who worked to make his family wealthy. If Hannah could play games, I decided I could, and headed through the crowd toward him.

I indicated we go outside, but he held his ground. "Okay, we can do this here." A look of disdain spread across his face, almost as visible as a tattoo. "Ask me what I do for a profession."

I was standing very close to him and he couldn't push me away without causing a scene.

"Tell me."

"I look after people; you know, look out for their interests. Mind them, you might say. Hannah gets the service for free. She doesn't like people who pester her."

"You're too young to be anything."

"Clever disguise, don't you think? I do not work alone; don't piss us off!"

I guess, in his privileged little world, he had never been challenged before, but truth to tell there were men like him in every class. Those who felt that women owed men something – just because they were men.

He stayed, but I could feel he was uncomfortable and he never let his eyes drift towards Hannah.

Aware that I had to get home and would have to catch the bus soon, she came to me at ten thirty. I told her the story and she burst into laughter. "My God," she said, "he'll think I've got connections to the Mafia. Let's hope he doesn't find out the truth." I asked her then if we could meet some time, and she told me no. "If you want to help me, Peter, don't ask questions. Treat it like it's a game where you might find answers one day, but not now."

*

On Saturday, Jenny, my middle sister, called up the stairs. "You've got another one on the phone; says her name is Natalie."

I couldn't remember giving her my number at the party and was curious. She asked me if I'd minded her calling me. Why would I object to a pretty girl giving me a call? I must admit, I didn't make it easy for her. She kept apologising for ringing and I wasn't saying much, maybe because I was taken by surprise. I think she was on the point of putting the phone down when I suddenly gained confidence and asked her if she would like to meet at The Old Duke for a drink at lunchtime the next day. I could sense the tension draining out of her voice and realised how hard it must have been for her to make the call. Nobody wants to be turned down, me included. I tried to summon up an image of her in my mind. She was shorter than me and blonde. My sisters, and most girls I knew, had auburn or brown hair. Try as I might, I could not visualise her face. Tomorrow would tell. The Old Duke was a music venue, but quiet on a Sunday lunchtime. It would be a good place to talk.

I expected her to arrive late. Hanging around waiting in a bar was bad enough for a bloke but for a young woman it was worse. I realised I should have organised things differently.

When she did arrive I was surprised. The light wasn't good at the party and my mind was elsewhere. I realised she would have pulled most men's eyes. I asked what she wanted to drink and she replied that she didn't want anything really, but would have a lemonade as she didn't want to be seen sitting empty-handed by the bar staff.

If there was a polar opposite to Hannah it was probably Natalie. She was curious about me and asked lots of questions about my sisters. She also talked a lot about herself and the people she knew. She was as open as Hannah was closed. I felt a fondness for her straight away and I wanted to know why she had contacted me. I asked her, and she was honest in her reply.

"I don't know really. You're not the type of guy I would expect to see with Hannah and I was curious, I guess."

"Was it Hannah who gave you my number?"

"Yes; she told me I'd find you interesting."

Although I could guess what Hannah's intentions were, I didn't care. I liked Natalie and wanted to know more. I asked where she lived and, when she told me, I was surprised. She only lived six streets away from mine. Her Catholic schooling meant our paths never crossed. She told me later that she had always been aware of me; I must have been blind not to have been aware of her.

Okay, Hannah, I thought, you wanted to distract me and you have succeeded. Perhaps too well, so you might have to wait the next time you need me.

We caught the same bus home and arranged to meet the following evening.

CHAPTER 4

Seth's new project was interesting. Working in different locations all the time was good. I used my lunchtimes to wander around and get to know the part of the city where we were working a little bit better. I had a good friend from school who worked in a caravan factory in the south of the city. He was there from 8.00 a.m. until 4.30 p.m. In deepest winter, he never got to see the sun. Dark when he left home and dark when he left the factory. He earned more money than me, but he was never going to start his own caravan factory; I was determined to have my own interior design business.

Every day I learnt more about the work, but more importantly I was beginning to understand client expectations, a trick Seth had learned a long time ago. Seth had a knack for choosing good clients, but he told me it hadn't always been so. The papers always go on about cowboy builders and rogue traders, but they never mention cowboy customers. The ones that ask for the best then try and knock you down. "Can we use cheaper material and cut costs in other ways?" they ask, while wanting the same quality of finish. You begin to get an instinct for late payers and those who won't pay at all.

"If you're not sure of a customer, Peter, just walk away."

Seth told me to read the newspaper Sunday supplements. Most of his clients got their ideas from them. Keep ahead of the game, he would say, and think how you can implement and improve on them. Sunday papers were expensive, but I managed to persuade family and neighbours to keep the supplements for me. I was too inexperienced to see how superficial most of it was. Seth knew and pointed me to the more interesting stuff. He was a mentor in his way, as was Joyce. However, a paint brush is a paint brush and at that stage I spent most of my time wielding one. Seth eventually realised I had the talent, and the much required patience, to match and hang expensive, heavily patterned wallpaper. As soon as he had confidence in me he left me to it and asked John and Cliff to join our little team to prep and undercoat the woodwork. Cliff's attitude had completely changed after Seth had told him I'd asked for him and John to be on the team. I wouldn't have if they hadn't been good enough; they both were.

To own a mock Tudor house facing on to Clifton Down you had to have money. I never found out what the guy did; he was only there on weekends. The client was lovely. Kate had good ideas, was appreciative, made us cake and brought us tea. We had come to see her as part of the team. This was rare; most clients accepted Seth but looked down their noses at the rest of us. If I sound like I've got a chip on my shoulder, I wouldn't blame you for thinking so.

It looked as though we had a steady few months in front of us, until John poked a hole in some dodgy-looking oak panelling and found the flowering body of a dry rot fungus. Seth called in the builder and dry rot specialists and we decorators moved three stories up to the loft.

All the wooden panelling was stripped from the hallway walls. It was oak, so the job had to be done with care. The best pieces were to be saved, treated and used again. Dry rot spores are everywhere, but they only take if the moisture level in the wood is right. The builder spotted a break in the damp-proof course. It had let enough moisture in to provide a cosy nursery for the dry rot spores to grow. He reckoned he could smell dry rot as soon as he entered a building.

Jeff the builder was full of stories of his life in the trade. His favourite always raised a smile. He told us that when he was young he was on an away team putting asbestos sheet roofs on engineering sheds in an army camp. When they arrived at their lodgings, Jeff was told he was to share with an old roofer called, Bill. Bill was a bit of a scruff, but although he liked the apple juice too much he was always steady on the girders. With a wry smile, the foreman told Jeff to hide his boots at night. Jeff paid scant attention to this warning until one day he got out of bed and found his boots full of something that smelled suspiciously like piss. After a night out, Bill had woken up in the early hours; still drunk and too desperate to reach the bathroom, he had relieved himself in Jeff's boots.

Jeff wasn't pleased, but still shed a tear when he heard later that Bill had taken a two-storey fall and died. His body was whole, but his bones were shattered, along with his heart. Scaffolding is compulsory now; it wasn't then. Working in the trade lets you see all sides of life. You also get to know death.

*

The first evening out with Natalie didn't go well. I guess we were both nervous, not really knowing what to expect of one another. We had gone for a walk, and the silences were growing longer. In a moment that could have turned the whole evening into a colossal disaster, I suggested we go to my home for a coffee or tea. My sisters were on her like a shot. Of course, they knew who she was. She was the girl who lived just a few streets away. My sisters inhabited a different world to mine and it was never more apparent than on the day they met Natalie, and closed ranks around her.

So, our first date consisted of a short walk and my sisters giving Natalie the 20 Questions. They were all there that night; Sally's boyfriend was working away and the other two were at a loose end.

Mum and Dad were watching telly and Sally was using the sewing machine in the front room, the room I'd foolishly hoped Natalie and I could occupy alone. That's how we all ended up together. Sally suggested I make tea for Natalie and while I was at it make some for everyone else, including Mum and Dad. Our house was one where the tea pot was never cold and no one ever turned down the offer of tea. It was always full of people: friends and boyfriends of my sisters, visiting aunts and cousins and friends of my parents. For most of my life, I had been the tiddler who swam among the bigger fish in a crowded bowl. The sudden appearance of a young female in my life was never going to go unnoticed. I really should have known better.

Odd as it may seem, that evening allowed our relationship to develop. Suddenly we had something to talk about. Natalie liked my sisters and said how nice she thought they were. 'Nice' and 'sister' were not words I used together very often, but I had to admit that was exactly the way they were with Natalie that evening. They didn't even try to embarrass me with tales of my childhood. I guess they thought me more than capable of embarrassing myself.

As I walked her home, she told me of her two older brothers and how she had always wanted a sister. Her brothers were keen rugby players and into sport in a big way. We met them at the gate to her house. She introduced me quickly. They didn't say much, just looked me over and headed for the front door. These were guys to whom the epithet 'boyish looks' would never have been applied. They looked as though they'd been shaving since they were ten.

I told her they seemed alright. Her reply was a little worrying. "They are very protective of me and I'll probably get the third degree when I go in. Don't be intimidated by them. They think they're being helpful but they can be really embarrassing."

I explained to her that sport wasn't my thing and she asked what I did like. I replied that I liked live music. Her eyes lit up and she asked what type of music. Anything apart from pop, I told her. We arranged to meet the following Friday to go to a modern jazz gig at The Arts Centre.

She wasn't the only one who got the third degree when arriving home. My eldest sister, Sally, was still working on the sewing machine in the front room and called me in. Sally never minced her words. "What happened to posh girl?" I explained that Natalie was a friend of Hannah's and it was Hannah who introduced us. Not that it was any of Sally's business, although she obviously thought it was. She just sighed and told me she had only just stopped thinking of me as her innocent little brother and now she had to think of me as a man. "Unfortunately, I have cause to know what men are like," she said. "Most of them are arseholes. Don't be like those, Peter: treat Natalie with respect." I mumbled something and once again sought refuge in my room.

*

On Tuesday evening, Caroline called me, saying Hannah was on the phone. Sally gave me one of her dark, disapproving looks. Hannah wanted me to accompany her on another jaunt the following weekend. Bearing in mind what big sister had told me, I mentioned that I was going to a gig with Natalie on Friday.

"Look," said Hannah, "Natalie and I are friends. She knows I have no interest in you the way she does and I'm just asking for your help." I told her, sorry, but if she wanted my help I'd need to know why. She told me this story...

"Since I turned twelve I've always had men trying to get close to me. Staying out of their way would mean locking myself away. I don't want to be a prisoner of my looks, Peter. I want to mix with interesting people, but the men want to get me into bed and the women see me as a threat. I can't help the way I look. For Christ's sake, I wish I'd been born different. I need someone to be my partner when I need one. I've talked to Natalie, and she sees what I'm up against. Ask her, Peter; she'll tell you it's okay."

I told her I would when I met Natalie on Friday and I could manage Saturday if I was needed. She laughed and told me I was even cooler than she'd thought. I didn't think so. I needed to talk this through with someone, and Natalie was the obvious choice.

*

The chemical boys had been and injected the walls with the poisons that would finish off the dry rot. The dampproofers turned up a day later to pressurise silicone into the gap in the damp-proof course. I kept out of the way. God knows what all that stuff they sprayed around did to them, but as sure as hell I wasn't going to let the stuff into my lungs.

The carpenters came next. They weren't the first and second fix sort you find on large sites. These were the guys the highly skilled joiners sent to fit their expensive oak panelling and wooden spiral staircases. The senior was a man called Rod; the apprentice was a guy called Leon. Rod seemed content to let Leon do most of the work, complaining that Leon would be ending his apprenticeship soon and he would have to start all over again with a novice. It didn't take me long to work out that Leon had passed the skill level of Rod, was quicker, and would probably set out on his own as soon as his apprenticeship was over. I liked him and soon discovered we shared a love of jazz. Turned out he was going to the same gig Natalie and I had planned to go to on the Friday.

CHAPTER 5

I caught the bus into town with Natalie. It was packed with people heading out to have a good time. The end of the working week; the time to go a little crazy. I went to the Glen dance hall once. Girls sat in tight circles or in groups dancing around their handbags, men eyeing them up while working out how best to approach the one they fancied and isolate her from the group. All accompanied by top-ten earworms that addled your brain for weeks. I could see the attraction, but it wasn't me. Anyway, at that time my boyish looks would have given me no advantage – more likely looks of scorn from both sexes.

Natalie was a little nervous at first, but the ice was broken when I noticed she was desperately trying to suppress a fit of giggles. I looked at her questioningly and she nodded toward a guy standing just three feet away from us on the crowded bus. I noticed some of the other girls were looking his way. He'd obviously spent a lot of time choosing his clothes and grooming himself before he went out. However, a last-minute trip to the loo had obviously left something undone, with a shirt tail poking out. Feeling for him, I called to him that he was flying without a licence. He looked angry at first then looked down and hurriedly pulled his coat around him. Shit, I thought – better to let him cover his embarrassment now than have the finger pointed at him all night. After all, it could so easily have been me.

The bus was crowded, so we couldn't talk much. When it reached the City Centre, the majority went one way and we went the other. A fifteen-minute walk took us to the Arts Centre and its relatively quiet bar. Leon was there with his girlfriend and called for us to join them. I left Natalie there and went to get drinks: her glass of lemonade and my glass of cider. When I was walking back toward the table I could see Natalie and Leon in animated conversation and his girl clinging a little closer to him. As I sat, I exclaimed, "Don't tell me, you two were at school together." Leon looked at me and asked how I knew. I replied that I could spot two Catholics in conversation from a mile away. Leon laughed and his girlfriend, Gill, visibly relaxed.

I met a guy on site once when we were painting the world with magnolia. I asked if he had any kids. Two daughters, he answered. No boys then, I asked. I did have one, he said, but we haven't spoken for sixteen years. "He insisted he marry his Catholic girlfriend. I told him that if he did I wouldn't speak to him again." His son did marry and he hadn't spoken to him since. I asked him if he regretted what he'd done. "Yes," he said, "it broke my wife's heart."

The band was a piano trio with a guest saxophone player. They were good. The pianist had obviously been listening to Bill Evans. The weak point was the drummer, who would have been more at home in a rock band. The sax player was a guy with a future. I know because I saw him many years later playing in Ronnie Scott's club in Soho.

When we talked in the interval, Natalie found a few things in common with Gill. The second set was much like the first, until the sax player decided to give us an extended solo improvisation in the style of John Coltrane. It was good, but he hadn't yet found enough in himself to make this style his own.

After it was all over, we shared a few drinks. Leon tried to convince me of the merits of early New Orleans jazz. He argued strongly that it was the root of most modern music. I couldn't disagree, as I guess I was as guilty as all the others who dismissed it as outdated without listening to it with a serious ear. He asked if we would like to go to a club he frequented the following Friday. I looked across at Natalie, and she nodded.

On the bus home, I broached the subject of Hannah. I told her I was going out with her the following evening and what she'd said about Natalie not minding. She turned and looked at me.

"Before I say more, tell me how you feel about her. I know some men become obsessed with her, so why aren't you?"

"I can understand how that happens, but for some reason I wouldn't think of having a relationship with Hannah any more than I would with one of my sisters. I'm curious about her, though. Please tell me what you know?"

"No more than you, I'm afraid. I met her at a friend's party and she explained her difficulties to me. She asked if I would mind going places with her. Maybe the men would think she was a lesbian and back off. I wasn't fazed by what she said and tried to help. We went out to some parties together, but it didn't work. She said she'd look for a man to help her. I didn't think she'd find one that wouldn't become obsessed with her. Then she found you."

"So, you know nothing about her family, or where she lives?"

"No, nothing, and I really don't mind if you help her, but please tell me if you start to feel differently."

I laughed, and told her I would. To lighten the mood, I asked Natalie what sort of music her brothers liked. She told me they didn't listen to music much and, when they did, it was Motown or whatever was in the Top Ten. Sport was the thing they lived for.

Our goodnight kiss at her gate had gained passion. I had no complaints.

When you're young and working-class, you tend to find out just how much you don't know when you somehow find yourself in middle-class circles. I didn't know then what I know now, and I quickly learned to shut my mouth when I was tempted to expose my naivety by saying something stupid. These were the circles that Hannah was taking me into. People who had holidayed abroad with their parents when they were young, studied a language, and had been to university. I had left school at fifteen and the only other country I'd been to was Wales, on a day trip to the Gower.

That Saturday with Hannah was my first experience of being totally out of my depth. We met in the centre of the city and took a bus to the east. It was a small house party, maybe six or seven couples and a few singles. None of them had an accent remotely like mine. They sounded like they were talking in another language and I came to realise that's exactly what they were doing. They were talking 'Middle-Class' and the only language I had was 'Working-Class'. I'd tried reading the Guardian once, but it might as well have been written in hieroglyphics; I just didn't have enough of the cultural references needed to make it meaningful to me. I do now, but not then. So I listened.

I didn't cling to Hannah, but I didn't move far from her. She appeared to be speaking middle-class fluently and, unlike me, was happily exchanging anecdotes about foreign places. The more she said the less I knew her.

I moved to the drinks table to fill my wine glass. I was developing a taste for red wine. Seth never kept beer at home and Joyce always offered me red wine when I went to their place. Seth drank nothing else. One of the single guys approached me. "Hi, I'm Howard."

"Peter."

"You seem very quiet, Peter."

"Do I?"

"Well, yes. Have you known Hannah long?"

"Why is it that every male we meet when I am out with Hannah asks me that question?"

"I am not sure what you mean."

"I think the real question you're asking is: what is a woman like Hannah doing with a guy like me? If so, you're asking the wrong person, but even if you asked the right one I don't think you'd get an answer you'd want to hear."

He looked a little nonplussed. I topped up my wine and moved back to Hannah's side. She was engaged with a couple in a conversation about university education and seemed to be enjoying herself.

I drifted through the rest of the evening, listening carefully to see if there was anything beyond the politeness of their chatter. At eleven, Hannah signalled that it was time to leave. I'd had more than enough by then. As we were putting on our coats to go, the guy Howard approached. "I'm off now; can I give you a lift anywhere?"

It took one brief look at Hannah's face for me to know her answer. I told him no.

"Are you sure?" he asked.

By this time, my patience had become as thin as fag paper. I asked him if there was something wrong with his hearing and gave him my sharpest look.

"Hey, no need to be aggressive."

I was beginning to get Hannah's situation. No doubt, as soon as we got in the car, he would have asked where we lived and it would have been, 'Okay, I'll drop you off first, Peter, as I live not far from where Hannah needs to be dropped off.'

I told him to fuck off, caught Hannah's arm and walked her away. I thought she might be upset by the way I'd acted, but as soon as we were far enough away she burst into laughter.

We caught the bus together to the centre of town. She told me she'd get a taxi from there and asked how I'd get home. I told her I'd walk. It would only take an hour or so and I needed to clear my head. She offered to pay for a taxi. I asked if she was an heiress in hiding; nobody I knew could afford taxis. She didn't give an answer, just said that it was better I walk as it would be good for me.

The bus wasn't as busy as it would be on the journey back from the Centre and we found a seat at the rear of the top deck. I told her of my conversation with Natalie the night before. She smiled.

"That's great, Peter; you can't guess what it means to me to have both of your support."

She asked me if I'd mind if she offered me a few tips. I didn't know where she was going with this, but agreed. She told me that if I was to be a successful designer I needed to study. "Go to the Central Library," she said. "Read about architecture, art, and even fashion. You need to immerse yourself in it if you're going to be a really good designer." She was right and I knew it. When we got off the bus, she kissed me lightly on the cheek. I walked to the taxi rank with her and waited until she was in the back of a cab. Then I turned away to make the long walk home.

On the way, I set to thinking. I was worried that I was beginning to see all men as predators. I knew they weren't and, on reflection, I could've been wrong about Howard. Hannah's worry about men was beginning to infect my thinking. Something must have happened to make her think the way she did. However, paranoid or not, I was going to continue to help her. Sooner or later I would know the story.

CHAPTER 6

We all knew that work at the mock Tudor house had to come to an end sometime. It made us a little sad as it was a joy to be working there. Seth's design had come together just as he had visualised it. He told us that we had worked really well as a team and he was looking for ways of taking Cliff and John on the cards permanently. It meant that I would have to take over the more technical side and deal with the customers when he was off drumming up work. It all sounded good to me. Now the carpenters had finished, it just left the ground floor hallway and dining room to be completed, before we moved outside.

Kate seemed pleased with everything. When Seth wasn't around, she always turned to me for advice, which did wonders for my confidence. We had all developed a soft spot for her. One morning when we were sat having tea, Cliff started complaining about his wife. He told us that she had expressed a liking for bone china. Cliff had seen a bone china mug with a picture of a dog on it. The picture reminded him of the little Jack Russell his wife was so fond of. Right, he thought, bone china and a picture of the dog she loves – I'll buy it. When he took it home, his wife unwrapped it and, with a mumbled thank you, put it in the kitchen cupboard.

Kate had listened while Cliff told his story and asked him where they were when his wife mentioned a liking for bone china. He told her that they were at a friend's. "Tell me, Cliff, can you remember what you were drinking out of when you were there?"

"Small mugs, I think; they had some sort of blue design on them."

"Well, Cliff, you were probably drinking out of bone china with a traditional Chinese blue design on it, and that is what your wife desired."

"Oh," said Cliff. Kate turned to look at the three of us.

"We women don't expect our men to be psychic, but we do expect them to pay attention."

The scaffolders turned up two days later. Guys with 'don't give me any bullshit' written all over their faces. Scaffolding was not for the likes of me. These are all-weather men who walk along slippery wet poles in the pouring rain at impossible heights. Men who wear thick leather gloves to stop their hands freezing to the metal when the temperature drops below zero. Nobody puts scaffold up for the scaffolders; they are men who take enormous risks to make us safe. It could be that they only took the work because there was no other, but I suspected some enjoyed the macho reputation that came with the job. I have never yet met a female scaffolder, though I don't doubt for one moment that they exist.

Gavin was six feet tall, broad in the shoulder and curt in speech. He was the boss and always turned up with his crews on the first day of a big job. Seth wanted to introduce me and explain that Gavin would have to deal with me on some jobs in the future. The big man looked down at me, seemingly measuring every inch that was missing for me to be tall enough to look him in the eye. I took a chance and asked him why all his trucks were named after Shakespeare characters.

"You read Shakespeare, boy?"

"Some," I answered.

"Then go away and read some more. You'll learn more from him than you ever learnt at school."

After that, I was ignored. I walked around the building and listened as Seth described what he wanted, while Gavin pointed out what was do-able and what wasn't. I was learning. I always thought that scaffolding wasn't that complicated – not true: it had to be wrapped around the building in a way that gave the best access for the painters. Knowing how this was done made a difference. Seth employed Gavin because he knew.

"You played a blinder there, Peter." Seth told me later. "Gavin is obsessed with Shakespeare. His wife told me once that he had a massive crush on his English teacher at school. A looker, so his mates told her. Gavin read Shakespeare until he could quote from it. After his crush was over, his love of Shakespeare remained. To be a mate of Gavin you have to show an interest. He'll like you now, but I suggest you start reading a sonnet a day so you can talk to him when you have to deal with the scaffold."

Kate treated the scaffolders just like us, inviting them in for tea and biscuits at the time we always took our break. Sometimes they joined us, sometimes not. It depended on the rhythm of their work. A painter can always stick his brush in a caddy of water and go for tea. Not so with those who have to make their work secure at each stage.

One day, they did make it down the scaffold to join us. One of them was about my age. Short, with broad shoulders and, unlike me, all muscle. I asked how he came to work for Gavin. His name was Donny and he told me this story…

"I left school with no qualifications and seemed to be drifting. The old man had a drinking friend with a scaffolding business. He hadn't been at it long and it was a pretty sketchy outfit. One day, we were working in one of the little towns to the south of the city. It was an old house whose front door opened right onto the pavement, so we had to park the truck on the other side of the road and carry the kit across. Luckily, the job was opposite a doctor's surgery with a forecourt where we could park. Dodging traffic with long poles was a bit of a pain. Terry, one of the older guys, decided it would be easier to carry the long poles upright. He got halfway across the road and the top of the pole hit a bare electric overhead supply cable. He fell to the ground and the pole narrowly missed a car. Terry wasn't moving and the boss was panicking. I ran to the surgery and called for help. A doc came out and started pushing on his chest. He saved Terry's life. After that, an ambulance and the police turned up. One of the coppers took the boss away for questioning and, after talking to the rest of us one by one, the other copper told us to pack up and go home. I thought I would never lift a scaffold pole again, but Gavin heard about it and told me he needed a quick-thinking lad. I've been with him ever since. He knows what he's doing and would never put us in danger. He told me nobody can be a scaffolder forever, so he's got me going to night school. I'm sort of enjoying it; wasn't ready for study when I was at school, but I'm ready now."

It seemed that Donny had a mentor in Gavin like I had in Seth. I would take a closer look at Shakespeare on my visit to the library. I felt an odd need to impress Gavin the next time we met.

*

I'd taken Hannah's advice and started going to the Central Library two evenings a week. Kate said I could keep a change of clothes at the Tudor house, so I went straight from work. The Central Library had a big art and architecture section. I had no idea where to start or what to look for. One of the assistants spotted my confusion She asked what I wanted and I told her I was interested in interior design. Her name was Margaret and she brought me a book about Candace Wheeler, who she claimed was the mother of modern interior design.

When you're young, you don't think the past matters much. I was learning that it did, and modern design was just a variation on a theme that Candace Wheeler and a few others had written about a long time ago. Lost in the past, I didn't hear the soft footsteps approaching from behind me. A hand on my shoulder brought me back.

"We were supposed to be meeting outside a quarter of an hour ago."

Natalie was standing in front of me, not looking pleased. I pulled her down into the seat next to me.

"Look at this, Natalie." She looked at the books spread out before me.

"They're nearly all written by women; what does that tell you?"

Natalie looked at me and smiled. "It means you need a woman's perspective. Now, get these back to where they belong and let's eat. I've booked us into our Spanish restaurant up the hill."

We were both still living at home so we could afford the occasional meal out and we took it in turns to pay. It had become routine, like our Friday night visits to the New Orleans jazz club with Leon and Gill.

"I'm worried about Hannah."

We'd ordered and were sipping our wine waiting for the meal to arrive.

"Hannah will ring when she wants something, Natalie; you know what she's like."

"No, I don't, and neither do you. That's what's so damn troubling."

"Sorry, Natalie, but what can I do about a woman who refuses to tell me where she lives, rings me from a public telephone box and makes a point of telling me we are playing some game?"

"I know all that, Peter, but she is real, a real woman and I know it's all weird, but I feel we ought to find out more about her. Will you help me?"

I looked across at her. What could I say? Natalie cared about everyone.

*

It's like some unwritten rule that all the time you're working inside, the sun is shining, but as soon as you move outside it either pisses down with rain or turns icy cold. This time it was the rain. Luckily, Seth had a few inside jobs to keep us busy until the weather changed.

John and Cliff were sent to join a small team Seth had working on a group of four new-builds. He had other plans for me.

Royal York Crescent is an architectural landmark in Bristol. Tall, five-storey, flat-fronted Georgian buildings with basements for servants, and kitchens and a mews in front of the cellars for stabling horses and grooms. The vaulted mews is covered by a promenade for the gentry to take the air. However, in the seventies it was not fully appreciated and had been hacked about by developers, turning its grandness into flats and student accommodation. Georgian splendour had become a crescent full of money pits. Seth had bought one for him and Joyce. He knew the way Bristol was going and could see just how gentrified the shabby student lets could become.

It's what we call a 'hospital job' in the trade. A long-term investment to send your guys to when the weather was bad or work was scarce. Seth had kept the students on three floors, but was near finishing the basement and the first floor. He wanted me to hang some wallpaper in the living room of the first floor flat that he'd planned to occupy himself. It was there, when I was sitting at the window eating my sandwiches, that I saw her go into next door. It was definitely Hannah, and she obviously had a key. I wasn't going to knock on the door; I'd wait and ask around first.

I asked one of the students if he knew who lived next door. He replied in the negative. He probably didn't notice much of what went on outside of his student circle. One of the female students might be a bit more curious. I made a point of sitting outside when I took a break so that people would be used to me being there.

One of the girl students came out to roll a fag and asked what I was doing in the flat. Decorating, I explained. "Could I see?" she asked. "I'm interested in design." I told her she'd have to finish her fag first. Seth hated the smell of tobacco and could detect even the slightest whiff of it. Her name was Melissa and she was studying French and Spanish. Duly impressed, she asked who the designer was. I told her it was her landlord. "A mate of yours?" she asked.

"Sort of," I replied. "We work together."

My hunch was right – Melissa was far more curious about her neighbours than the guy I'd spoken to. Apparently, Hannah lived alone in the basement flat, and an old woman – she thought might be her grandmother – lived on the first floor. The only other occupant was an older man who lived in a separate apartment at the top of the building. I asked how she knew all this and she told me that she had got to know the old woman's cleaner when they were both outside smoking. Apparently, Melissa's flatmates disliked the smell of cigarettes so much they made her go outside to smoke. I was brought up encased in the smell of fag smoke so it didn't bother me. Only ever took a drag on one, though. Coughed for an hour and that was it. Never bothered again.

"Nobody knows much about the woman in the basement," Melissa said, "but all the men here drool over her. Not surprising, really; she's a bit of a looker. The cleaner is never asked to clean her apartment. She only cleans for the old woman and the man in the loft. Apparently, the old lady is the last person alive to receive a pension from the East India Company. She must be really ancient if that's true."

I asked if she knew if the woman in the basement worked. "If she does," she told me, "it's a job that doesn't require regular hours. She seems to come and go as she

pleases. You're not beginning to drool over her are you?"
I told her she was not my type. She asked me who was,
and I told her a blonde girl I spent my spare time with. "A
pity," she said, smiling, as she headed for the stairs.

I wasn't due to meet Natalie until the following
evening. My news could wait until then. I knew that a
phone call would lead to lots of questions I couldn't
answer, so best to talk about it face-to-face.

*

The next morning, I was setting up the pasting table when
there was a ring on the doorbell. I ignored it. Seth had a
key, so it wouldn't be him and I wasn't expecting anyone
else. It was quiet for a while and then there was loud
knocking on the apartment door. Luckily, I hadn't started
to paste the wallpaper I'd begun to unroll. I wasn't in a
hurry when I walked to the door, but the person outside
obviously was. I opened it and there stood Hannah.

"Thank God it's you."

She was not her usual calm self. I just looked at her
waiting for an explanation.

"What are you doing here?"

I didn't answer, just led her into the flat. Once inside,
I told her Seth was the new owner of the building and I
was there working. She looked around.

"Of course you are. Sorry, Peter. but when the cleaner
told me that someone had been asking about me I wanted
to know who."

"Hannah, if you don't mind me asking – just how the
hell did you get to be so fucking paranoid?"

The look in her eyes wasn't shock; it was hurt.

"I saw you go in the other day and just asked one of the students if they knew you. I didn't knock on your door because, well, you wanna keep your life a big secret – then carry on. However, when it impinges on mine, expect a reaction."

I told her that Natalie was worried about her and wanted to know if she was okay.

"Sorry, Peter; when are you seeing Natalie next?"

"Tomorrow. We are going to eat at El Roble after my study time at the library."

"Come to my place instead. I'll have something ready by eight."

"You're sure?"

She didn't reply to my question, just asked to see what I was doing.

I showed her around the flat, but she didn't seem impressed. I'd see why the next day when we got a look inside her apartment. She left without the usual pretend kiss on both cheeks. I hated that stuff anyway. Nobody else I knew acted like they were French. Working-class men and women just didn't do that sort of thing back then.

CHAPTER 7

Natalie arrived at the Central Library early enough for us to take a steady stroll up to Royal York Crescent. I'd had to phone her in the end so she could cancel our table at El Roble.

I brought her up to date with what I knew, which wasn't much. She told me she was getting fed up with her job and asked if I'd mind if we studied design together at the library. I wasn't sure about her motives but I liked her company and it would be good to have someone to bounce ideas off.

As we approached Hannah's, I could see Melissa sitting on the steps of next door's entrance smoking one of her roll-ups. She gave Natalie the once-over, then turned to me.

"So, there really is a blonde in your life."

Natalie turned to look at me as I replied, "Melissa, this is Natalie; Natalie, this is Melissa."

"Pleased to meet you," said Natalie.

"Can't say the same," said Melissa. "I was rather hoping you were a figment of his imagination." With this, she smiled and went towards the door.

"Who was that?" Natalie asked.

I told her she was a student who enjoyed winding me up.

"I bet if I went in there now and knocked on her door it would be a boyfriend who answered it." Natalie laughed and told me she'd met her type before.

On the front door there was a bell pull and a more modern electric bell push clearly marked 'basement'. I pressed it and, after a while, Hannah opened the door. She led us into the hallway and to a door beneath the grand staircase which opened onto stairs leading down to the basement. Dozens of paintings covered the walls. I knew what prints looked like and these weren't prints. They were oils, watercolours and charcoal sketches. At a guess, all originals, but there was no theme: abstract next to portrait next to primitive. Art was a new subject to me, but I had grasped enough to know what I was looking at.

The living room was warm, cosy even. Sofas of bright patterns scattered with cushions of many, but subdued colours. Bare floorboards covered by rugs that obviously hadn't been made locally. I don't know what I expected, but a log fire in the hearth and the warmth it gave made it hard to feel anything other than relaxed.

Hannah was dressed in jeans with a loose woollen top over a plain white T-shirt. She gave me a glass of red wine and Natalie a glass of white, then led us to the rear of the large sitting room to where a table had been set for three. She asked how my studies at the library were going and I told her they were going well. I didn't tell her that Natalie had decided to join me; that was for her to say. We had some tomato on small pieces of bread, which Natalie told me later was called bruschetta. I rather liked them. After a little more small talk, Hannah fetched a dish from the kitchen. She explained it was her version of the Greek dish moussaka. Not the sort of food I was used to, but tasty. Hannah brought more wine and a variety of cheese. Then she began to talk.

"I promised myself I was going to be honest with you. I need to be. Both of you have helped me and never pushed for explanations. The other day, Peter, you asked me why I was so paranoid; maybe what I say now may help you understand."

This is what Hannah told us.

"I am descended from pirates. No, don't laugh, Peter; hear me out. There was much greater wealth in my family than there is now. You must have heard how British privateers attacked Spanish and Portuguese vessels during the sixteenth century. They did so with the blessing of the monarch and were rewarded with land and knighthoods. You can read all about it in the library.

"The men in my family didn't stop there. From robbery on the high seas they turned to robbery by other means. To cut a very long story very short, they were later involved in the East India Company which, with its own huge army and navy, laid the basis for the British Raj. It's a long history and one where money was lost and regained. Many of the large country houses scattered around Britain were built on the wealth gained during that period. My grandmother comes from that side of the family. Granddad's family had a less colourful background and it wasn't until he had control of the family business that it became a major company in the chemical sector. Eventually, he was bought out, but retained large shareholdings which gave him a seat on the boards of those companies he retained an interest in."

"So, how does all this connect to you?" Natalie asked.

"The woman upstairs is my grandmother. Her husband, my grandfather, was Lord Roxford, who was given a life peerage for services to industry. Nana is a descendent of one of the key players in the East India Company and some of that money came to her. My family lost a lot of money in the Wall Street Crash, but still owned a lot of property. Their son, my father, married a young refugee from Poland. They were killed in a rail crash in Switzerland before I had real memories of them. I was brought up here in my grandmother's house."

Hannah paused and took a sip from her wine. I didn't know quite what to say. Natalie said how awful it must have been for her to lose her parents. Hannah sighed and explained that it was hard to miss people you never really knew. There was just an ache where they should have been. It was just other people's memories and photos. If her grandmother hadn't reassured her that they really were her parents, they could have been anyone.

I was listening closely and somehow feeling glad that I didn't have the complicated family stuff that Hannah had to deal with. Hannah went on.

"The result of this is that, when I came of age, I inherited my father's wealth, and when Nana dies I will inherit hers. Peter, you once jokingly asked me if I was an heiress. Well, I'm not one in that old cheesy way we think of them, but my wealth has made me very wary of men. Years ago, marriage meant you became a chattel of your husband, along with everything you possessed. You'd think that right now, in the nineteen seventies, things would be different. Not so: marriage still gives your husband the upper hand. My first degree was in law. Nana suggested it; she has always worried that some man would try and gain control of my inheritance. Like I said, things are changing, but it's still a man's world out there."

When you've got nothing worth worrying about, the sort of stuff that preoccupies Hannah doesn't cross your mind. Nonetheless, I could see where she was coming from. I asked her what she was studying now and she said she travelled up to Oxford most weeks as she was doing a postgraduate degree in sociology, focusing on the study of crime. Christ, I thought to myself, how does a woman so elegant and intellectually bright get to see herself as being cursed. I was beginning to learn that money doesn't necessarily bring freedom, especially for women.

I turned to look at Natalie, who was looking very thoughtful, but not saying much. Then to Hannah.

"I sort of get it, Hannah. You don't want anyone taking control of your life. Falling for someone could be an easy way of getting screwed." She laughed. "Financially, I mean, Hannah." She laughed even more and turned to Natalie, telling her that she just didn't know how lucky she was. Well, it's all relative. We spent the rest of the evening talking about family. We told Hannah we would try to be there for her when she needed us.

I didn't think Hannah quite had it right about me and Natalie. We were growing together bit by bit, but we were still unsure of each other. I felt Natalie was trying harder than me.

*

The rain had stopped and I was back on the scaffold with John and Cliff. John had drawn the long straw and was just ahead of us, opening the casement windows and coating the closing edges.

Since we started working as a team, Cliff had more or less kept himself to himself and I hadn't made much of an effort to engage with him. John had, and it had begun to nag at me. Cliff wasn't a really bad bloke, but he was bloody hard to warm to.

I asked if he had always been a painter. He told me no. Some people can be really good at hiding what's bothering them and I guessed that Cliff was one of these. He wasn't going to say much that day so I didn't push it. It looked like we were all in it for the long haul with Seth. It would take a while, but brick by brick I would try and pull down the wall that separated Cliff and me.

John was another matter. Tea breaks would often start with, "Did I tell you the one about..." Always cheerful, his mood only broke at the mention of an obvious injustice. John was a socialist. Not a communist, he would adamantly add, but a socialist. He hated the Tories and hoped Labour would form a government after the next general election. I always listened closely to what John had to say and I guess that in a way he was another mentor. Seth never argued with John, just claimed that all governments made it hard for small businesses.

According to John, Seth had the gift of the gab and would always come up smelling of roses. I thought there was much more to Seth than that. His politics didn't stretch to socialism, but he was fair-minded and tried to do what he could.

*

Friday found Natalie and me in the long room above the bar in The Ship Inn. The band was playing St Louis Blues and, as usual, the out-of-tune double bass grated on my ears. The prematurely white-bearded trombone player played his part skilfully, while the clarinet player wove around the trumpet player's rendition of the melody. These musicians, with the exception of the bass player, had to be admired for their dedication to a purist version of early jazz.

We were supposed to be meeting Leon and Gill and it looked like they were not going to turn up. I was on my second pint and finally into the music when Leon arrived alone. One look at his face and I knew the evening was going downhill from there. Gill had ditched him and he wasn't happy. I'm not good at the consoling business but Natalie obviously was. I drifted in and out of the tale as I was listening to the music. It was the age old, he didn't understand her stuff. Natalie wanted to know why Gill felt the way she did. Leon pointed out that if he knew maybe she wouldn't have ditched him.

I'd listened to my sisters moaning about their boyfriends enough to know that if a woman has convinced herself that her boyfriend wasn't paying her enough attention there was no point in trying to make her see differently. Leon didn't see it coming, so I guess that's why he was really pissed off.

The evening seemed to drag on, with Leon crying on Natalie's attentive but metaphorical shoulder. I was glad when the band announced the last number before signing off. Appropriately, it was a blues.

Fortunately, we were heading in a different direction to Leon. I thought the subject could be left behind but, no, I had obviously done something to upset Natalie. We sat on the bus together with an uncomfortable quietness between us. I asked what the problem was. Natalie asked why I had been so unsympathetic towards Leon. I tried to explain. I mean, what could I say; going over and over things doesn't always help. I'd seen my sisters getting through a rejection: first tears, then frustration, then anger, then sod that, he wasn't worth it anyway. Leon would get over it. All this was said, of course, with the wisdom of someone who hadn't gone through a break-up. An experience I was beginning to think I wasn't far away from. What is the right answer when someone asks you why you lack empathy?

I care about people; of course I do, but I never get involved unless I can do something real to help. Leon was never going to cry on my shoulder like he did on Natalie's. We'd have probably just got pissed together and gone our separate ways.

*

Natalie didn't turn up the following Wednesday. I rang on Thursday, but one of the brothers told me she wasn't in. I should have rung again, but I knew instinctively I'd be wasting my time. I wasn't going to follow Leon down the bog hole of rejection. I liked Natalie; she was good company and good to talk to and maybe in those two phrases were the reasons why it would never have worked out. I was told on our second date that she didn't believe in sex before marriage. I wasn't bugged by this, but maybe I was meant to be. I began to worry that there really was something wrong with me.

I talked to Sally about it and she was honest enough to tell me that she thought it would never have worked. Sally didn't think I was the right one for Natalie. I left a note by the phone saying that if Natalie should ring I was out. She did ring, but it was a lot later. The one really positive thing to come out of my break-up with Natalie was that I would never again have to listen to that God-awful bass player at the club on Fridays.

Three weeks later, my sister Caroline told me that Hannah had rung. This time she'd left her number. I rang her that evening and she asked if I would like to come for supper after my studies at the library. I didn't know what she meant by supper; I assumed it was a meal. In our house it was a cheese and tomato sandwich an hour before going to bed.

I arrived about eight and was glad to get out of the cold, damp evening. No sign of Melissa this time. Hannah opened the door dressed much as she was the last time. We went downstairs to the cosy sitting room and sat opposite one another on the sofas.

"It's just you and me. I thought you might need cheering up."

"You heard, then?"

"Yep, Natalie rang to tell me she'd split with you and she was seeing someone called Leon. She couldn't be there for me anymore."

"Well, the Leon bit is news, but I can't say I'm surprised. Apparently, I lack empathy. Leon must have some, I guess."

Hannah gasped in surprise. "What! Is that what she said?"

"Well, poor old Leon was gutted at being rejected by his girl. Apparently, I was insufficiently sympathetic. Looks like Natalie had enough for both of us."

Hannah smiled. "When I look back, I don't see how you put up with me, but you did. You don't lack empathy, Peter, but maybe you do know a lost cause when you see one. Let's eat – I've made a casserole to warm us up."

This was probably the first time I felt really relaxed in Hannah's company. I told her stories of growing up with three sisters. She was envious. I told her she shouldn't be. Her grandmother insisted she be home-schooled. Hannah thought she would have hated boarding school anyway and didn't mind being taught at home. Her grandmother could afford the best tutors and she really benefited from it, gaining a genuine love of learning from tutors passionate about their subjects. However, she would have loved brothers or sisters.

She told me a story of when she first came of age and realised she had a seat on the board of a London company. She was determined to take up her place. When she arrived at her first meeting, she was surrounded by men in suits. Patronising, misogynistic, condescending; three new words for me to store. She explained that they thought she could be easily manipulated; she couldn't. The result was various factions trying to get her on side. However, her grandmother had schooled her well. She only travelled to London for board meetings and avoided the social interaction between board members. Nevertheless, she had three marriage proposals within the first year.

This was a world I knew nothing of. It made me think of John and his socialist ideas. I wondered what he would have made of Hannah; perhaps he was too sensitive to see her as the poor little rich girl. It was gone midnight when Hannah organised a taxi. She knew the driver and told him to charge my fare to her account. We'd sat chatting about our lives like old friends. Sometimes, I had to ask for translations of the long words that slipped into her side of the conversation and sometimes she had to ask what I meant when I told her something in working-class.

I don't think she'd meant for me to stay so long and I certainly hadn't, but somehow it happened. When I told her I had to go because I needed to be up at the crack of sparrow fart, she burst into laughter.

*

Cliff was still not saying much, so he took me by surprise one morning. John was ahead of us on the scaffolding and out of earshot. "Can we stop a minute, Peter?"

"Sure."

"I owe you an apology."

"For what?"

"Come on, Peter; I was a bit of a bastard when we first met. I've seen how you work and I can see why Seth thinks so highly of you. You could have easily dropped me in it, yet you didn't and instead recommended me for this job."

"Okay, Cliff, let's leave all that behind us. You know your stuff and I wouldn't have recommended you otherwise."

Things settled between us after that. He told me about his past. A Borstal Boy, reformed and made good. No thanks to the local borstal, though. All it gave him was the courage it took to get through his time there. A petty crime and an unsympathetic magistrate was all it needed for a kid to be sentenced to spend time in a borstal. He swore he'd done nothing wrong, just been in a department store in the centre of the city at the wrong time. He'd seen a few lads acting suspiciously and watched as security moved in on them. Engrossed in what was going on, he'd failed to notice the guard move in behind him. He was dragged to a room and interrogated by a security guy. Cliff wasn't worried. He'd done nothing wrong. The security guy was obviously pissed off and, when the police came, he claimed he'd found something in Cliff's coat.

"A fucking bar of diabetic chocolate, for fuck's sake; what the hell would I want with that?"

The copper told Cliff he knew his sort, the sort who would steal anything – just for the hell of it. The magistrate obviously agreed and, despite good character references, sent him off to borstal for three months. His mother was a chapel-goer until the day he was sentenced; couldn't face it after that. His father believed him and threatened violence to anyone who suggested Cliff wasn't innocent, which didn't help. One pissy security guard managed to poison Cliff and his family's lives. When a man gets handed that sort of shit, you can understand why a candle of anger constantly burns inside him. The silence was broken and, even though Cliff was years older than me, a bond was growing. When I told John about it, he looked me in the eye and said, "About bloody time."

Comradeship is not friendship – it's different; it's something that bonds working men and women together in their workplace, in their common struggle to face whatever the day shoves at them. Cliff and I might never be close friends, never visit each other's houses or go drinking together, but we would be comrades, and that's as close a bond as any.

*

Sally had invited her boyfriend around for Sunday lunch. It was the only meal in the whole week when we all managed to eat together. A quiet day for ritual hair-washing among the sisters and the anticipation of escape for me as soon as eating was over. Today was different. I could sense it. All the sisters were at their best. I'd met Sally's boyfriend, Graham, a few times and I obviously fell below the bar set for people who needed to be impressed. Mum was fussing and I'd thought that, if she didn't know what was coming, she'd guessed. A sort of awkwardness disappeared when Dad spoke up. Dad lived in a maelstrom of femaleness and his voice was rarely heard above it. Today, he was transformed into the master of ceremony.

After we'd eaten, Dad announced, "Graham came to me and asked for Sally's hand last week. I said I'd consult with you all, then Sally would do what she wanted anyway. Well, what do we say?"

Dad had done something he rarely did: he'd made a joke. It was the sign of approval Sally wanted but didn't need. Nobody said anything, so I spoke up.

"Welcome to the family, Graham. If you want survival lessons, just ask."

Sally gave me a jokingly disapproving look. After that, everyone joined in congratulating them.

The phone started ringing in the hallway and Caroline went to answer it. She called me. It was Hannah. She was obviously upset and asked for me to come straight away. She'd send a taxi. I didn't get a chance to ask what was troubling her. I made my excuses and went outside to sit on the wall and wait.

CHAPTER 8

There were no lights on in the basement when I arrived. I rang the bell, but there was no answer. Hannah had to be upstairs with her grandmother. I rang the house bell and eventually the old gent who lived on the top floor came to answer it.

"You are Peter?" the old gent asked.

"Yes, Hannah rang; is everything okay?"

"Lady Roxford has taken a fall and will not let Miss Hannah fetch an ambulance. I fear there is little I can do to help. I'll take you to them."

If the basement was cosy, the first floor apartment was anything but. I was led to the sitting room which had a tall ceiling, massive ceiling rose and carved cornices running around the room. From picture rails hung an assortment of portraits. It was formal, almost like something from a period drama on the TV.

When Hannah came into the room, she was not smiling. She kept her distance as she explained, "I'm sorry, Peter. I panicked. It's Nana; she fell in her bedroom. The servants' bell from there to the basement is still working and she managed to reach it. Her doctor is coming but he could be another hour. He's the only one she trusts. I need to get her into bed as she's in a lot of discomfort."

"Let's do it, then."

"Wait, I'll go in first and tell her you're here." Two minutes later, Hannah reappeared.

"Peter, she knows about you, but she will be unsure. Please do what you can."

I'd never seen a four-poster bed before and had always associated them with vulnerable women and vampires. This one was huge, and on the floor next to it was sitting a much older version of Hannah. She looked up at me.

"Hannah has told me about you. Do you think you can lift me into my bed?"

It was odd; I've never thought myself strong, but I wasn't that weak. She may once have been as striking as Hannah, but now she looked frail and small. I didn't think much more. Just told her to lift her knees, then knelt and put one arm under them and the other behind her back. There was nothing to her. She sat upright on her bed, and looked a lot more comfortable."

"Thank you, Peter."

"It's nothing; are you more comfortable now?"

She looked at her granddaughter and smiled. "Fetch us some wine, dear. What does Peter like?"

"Are you sure, Nana? Dr Marston will be here soon and you know how he disapproves of alcohol."

"Blast, Dr Marston. I am old enough to know what's good for me and what's not."

Before Hannah reappeared with some wine, I found myself being gently questioned by the old lady. She'd managed to extract quite a lot of information by the time Hannah returned. A sharp woman, I thought, not one to be messed with. When the bell rang and the doctor was announced, I was glad to escape to the basement. It was a while before Hannah came to join me.

"How is she?" I asked.

"No bones broken, but a lot of bruises. She has never fallen before. I'm really sorry, Peter, but my first instinct was to call you. I really hope you don't mind."

"I didn't mind, but I was curious as to why she felt there was no one else she could call on."

"No, Peter. You must have seen the state the Crescent is in. Poorly maintained, student bedsits both sides and even a squat at the end of the rank. When Nana moved here it was the grandest place in Bristol. She has too many happy memories to think of moving. Students move in and out all the time and the whole Crescent seems to have a transient population nowadays."

"Have you no friends you could've asked?"

"None I trust, and it would take time to explain why; essentially, you are the only one who really knows me. I mean, knows what I am and what I have. Nana always told me to be careful who you let into your life because some of them will never let go once they know you have money. I've come to think that you are not someone like that."

She asked me what would happen if there was a sudden illness in my family. I laughed and asked, "You mean something my sisters couldn't deal with? To be honest," I told her, "there is not one neighbour in our short street we couldn't call on and who wouldn't respond immediately. We all have our problems; solidarity is how we cope."

I asked about the old man who'd let me in and Hannah told me he had been her nana's driver for years and had no family of his own, so when he was due for retirement she moved him into the flat upstairs. He's devoted to Nana, she said, but too old to be of much help now.

I was thinking about the long walk home and that I'd better shift my arse if I was to get some sleep before the alarm clock rang. It was then Hannah asked for a favour. There was a spare bedroom in the basement – would I stay just in case the old lady fell again? I looked her in the eye and asked if she was really that worried. She didn't respond, but I could see she was. I told her I would, but I'd need to ring home; they'd be worrying otherwise. She smiled and pointed to the phone.

If you think all this improbable, you wouldn't be on your own. Looking back on it, I think I might have, but, improbable as it might seem, it was happening. Hannah had fallen into a fearsome trap between her money, her needs, and the men she feared might exploit her. Somehow, I'd turned up in armour I couldn't remember having polished. To say Hannah confused me would be putting it lightly. Confident enough to take a degree or two and ask a painter to take her out, but vulnerable in so many other ways When and how does falling for someone begin? I was watching myself for the symptoms.

Luckily the Tudor house was only a short walk away from Hannah's place in Clifton. There'd been no calls in the night so, as soon as light shone through the curtains, I was up and away. I'd call Hannah later if she didn't ring me first. Luckily, my working clothes were still at the Tudor house from Friday. I had abandoned the jazz club at The Ship in favour of the Central Library.

I arrived to find Seth had turned up on site. He told me not to change. I was to go with him to look at another big job. A house belonging to a friend of our current client. She'd seen our work and was keen for Seth's opinions about what she could do with the house she'd just moved into.

It was in Westbury on Trym. The Trym brook actually ran through the garden, which was surrounded by a high stone wall. We entered the garden through large wooden gates. Once inside, you could imagine you had left the city for the countryside. Across the veg plots and lawns we were faced with a very large building that must have once been the house of a wealthy farmer.

As we walked towards the old oak front door, Seth told me that this was going to be a learning project for me. He wanted me to listen closely to what the client had to say and come up with some ideas and sketches. If he used them, I would see the results in my wage packet.

This client wasn't so easy-going, but I'd learnt from life that everyone expects to get ripped off until they come to know and respect you. Especially when you have a working-class accent. Introductions and survey over, Seth drove me back to site and my paint brush.

*

For the first time, I decided to take the initiative with Hannah.

I rang her that evening and, before she could say anything, I asked how her grandmother was. She replied that she was back to her old self. Good, I said, then told her I owed her a few meals and would like her to 'accompany me' to El Roble the following Friday. She thanked me, but told me she had to be in Oxford for a meeting on Friday and wasn't sure what time she would get back. Would I like to come to her flat for a meal on Wednesday? I mentioned El Roble again, but she said she liked to cook and, if I didn't mind, we could eat in.

I tried to sort all this out in my head. Was this a date? A thank you dinner for helping with her grandmother, or just a meal with a friend? I decided it had to be the latter. If there was going to be anything else, it would have to come from her. My friendship cap would have to sit on my head for now.

*

Melissa was outside as I was walking towards Hannah's, dragging on the last of her roll-up.

"What happened to blonde girl, then? Posh girl taken her place?"

I told her I didn't need advice, nor did I need her nose in my life. She laughed.

"My God, if you've linked up with basement woman you'll have all the men around here dying of envy. There's a party down at the squat on Saturday. Why don't you both come? Some good musicians are playing."

"Playing what?" I asked.

"Folk rock, I think. It's open house, so you won't need an invite."

"We'll see."

"Hope you do; you sound like a couple who'd title a folk song: The Painter and the Basement Girl."

Melissa was undoubtedly finding me a useful subject for honing skills as a wind-up merchant. Thinking about the party, I decided I would mention it to Hannah.

When Hannah came to the door, she gave me a hug and one of her annoying air kisses. I wasn't going to complain; her softness stirred something in me that raised my body temperature. She told me her nana was waiting to see me upstairs. She wanted to thank me.

The sitting room was how I remembered it. Nana was sat in her chair with a stick hanging over the arm. She was upright and using her green eyes to give me the once-over. "Hannah tells me you work in design."

I wasn't going to mislead the old girl.

"Yes, for my mentor, Seth. He's bought the student house next door and hopes to restore it."

"He's not going to be another student landlord is he?"

"No, he believes that the city is changing and these houses will once again become what they were."

"Goodness, Peter, you have cheered me up. I would like to meet your mentor as he's to be my neighbour."

I told her that I was sure Seth would like to meet her and I would arrange something and let Hannah know. She thanked me for the other night. Hannah told her our food would be ready and we left for the basement.

Hannah thanked me for being so polite. I told her that it would be difficult for me to be anything else as I was brought up to respect those who carried the weight of age on their shoulders. My granddad always said, "Respect your elders and in return you'll learn what they know. You might even learn it several times, as they tend to repeat themselves, but if you don't listen you'll come to regret it."

There was no doubt: Hannah was a good cook. All was prepared and a fish based pasta dish was put straight in the oven. I was told that it was layered lasagne with a cream sauce and flaked fish. One of her nana's favourites. Apparently, Hannah cooked for her sometimes and froze meals for when she was away for her nana to defrost in her kitchen upstairs.

Definitely not the meat and three veg I was used to, but something I could get used to if given the chance. Hannah had discarded the wine I'd brought in favour of one she had decanted earlier. Spanish, she told me and made me repeat the word Rioja several times until I'd pronounced it correctly.

We fell easily into one another's company.

I told her about my encounter with Melissa and the invite to the gig at the squat. She thought for a while then told me that if I was up for it she would like to go.

"Alright," I said, then explained that if Melissa was right I might have to spend the whole evening keeping potential admirers away from her.

She laughed. "You seem to be good at that," she told me. "Let's go and see what happens."

*

I spent the next two evenings drawing up sketches and ideas for the new client. It was not an easy project as it was an old cottage type of building which the client obviously wanted fitted out with modern conveniences. They also wanted to keep as many of its historical features as possible. I had spent all my time in the library studying modern design. I wasn't sure where to start with this type of project, until about 10 o'clock on Friday evening, then it came together and I knew what I would give to Seth on Monday.

Hannah had rung earlier and asked if I was still keen on going to the party. She suggested I come to her place on the Saturday afternoon. She'd make some food for us before we left. She also had some ideas about how we might dress to go. She told me to come wearing denims and a T-shirt. Turned out she had been observing the squat dwellers and those who sympathised with them. We arrived, with her wearing a granny dress and me wearing my denims and a denim jacket over my white T-shirt. I was definitely not going to wear the brightly patterned flowery shirt she'd found for me.

We had just got through the door into the crowded hallway when Melissa spotted us and made her way towards us. A tall guy with a Zapata moustache followed in her wake.

"You made it, then."

"Hannah, this is Melissa, the malicious gossip I told you about."

Melissa laughed and told Hannah she was pleased to meet her. Hannah just nodded a reply. I could see she wasn't keen on engaging with her. Unperturbed, Melissa insisted she be our guide and I whispered to Hannah to let her show us around. She probably knew everyone there and all about them. It would be a quick way of deciding how long we wanted to stay. As I expected, the place was in a sad state of repair. Walls covered with faded Victorian patterned paper and green and brown paint, most likely full of lead. Some of the squatters had obviously tried to make their rooms homely, but everyone there was transient and they knew it. It was a cheap roof over their head, but a temporary one. In the large sitting room on the first floor some musicians had begun to play. It was all acoustic. I was informed enough to know who

Bert Jansch was and I knew the guys playing were under his influence. A new English folk style which I liked immediately.

We didn't get to stop for long. Melissa dragged us up the stairs to the room directly above the one we had just been in. It was a makeshift studio which was obviously being used by more than one artist. Hannah was more curious than me and stopped in front of a tall painting. It was a portrait of a naked female in black and white, which looked as if it had been made out of thousands of tiny black dots. Hannah asked who the artist was. Melissa thought it might be a guy called Graham Bayley, but wasn't sure. She said she'd find out.

The air was thick with the smell of tobacco and weed and it was clear from the mumblings from one of the rooms we passed that the glassy-eyed people within were spaced out on something else. I'd heard about LSD, but didn't know how to spot the symptoms. Sitting around staring into space wasn't my idea of socialising, so we made our way back down to the music. After a while, Melissa gave up trying to pump Hannah for information and left us listening to a woman with an angelic voice. I only got to know her name years later when I was listening to a folk compilation and recognised the voice straight away.

We left around ten. By that time, we'd both had enough. It was Hannah's idea. She suggested we go back to hers and open a bottle of wine. It ended up being two; time seemed weirdly suspended when we were in each other's company. It was then that I told her this might be our last evening together. She didn't show surprise, just asked why. I told her that I had been monitoring myself for the symptoms other men have when they are around her and the news wasn't good.

She looked a little sad then told me to be patient. "Let's just keep it going for a little longer. I don't want to lose you, Peter; I really don't. Our evenings together, well, I treasure them. Please let me think."

I was realistic. I would soon know whether she had any feelings for me. We had certainly grown closer than I thought we ever would. I told myself to get real and go and buy a new paintbrush or something.

*

Seth called in first thing on the Monday to pick up the envelope with the sketches and ideas I had for the Westbury farmhouse. He dropped off a young lad called Dougie who, as Seth explained, I was to take under my wing. A distant relation of Joyce, he was gangly and uncoordinated. My first impressions weren't positive, but Seth was a good judge of people, so I did the best I could to put him at ease. As it turned out, it was John's wing he ended up under. It's not good to knock over a freshly opened can of paint on your first day at work. John reassured him and began to teach him what he needed to know. The lad also brought out a fatherly side in Cliff that I'd never seen before. I was relieved and left them to it.

The following day, Seth picked me up from home first thing, and we went back to the office he shared with Joyce. They'd both taken a good look at my plans.

The first thing Seth wanted to know was why I had suggested knocking out the small window in the dining room and replacing it with much bigger French casements. I explained that, while I thought the farmhouse cosy with lots of original features, it lacked light. Putting French casements into the large kitchen diner would bring light into what I guessed would be the most used room in the house. It would be opposite the dining table where people could sit and look out onto the garden. I hadn't wasted too much time on the kitchen units as I knew this was something that Seth would design with the joiner he used to make bespoke kitchens. Ikea had not yet reached our shores and the age of the flat pack kitchen had only just begun.

Cottages are dark places with small windows designed to keep the warmth in and the winter out, which is why I had suggested light colours for most of the rooms. Seth was curious as to why I had not suggested fixed wall lights. Personally, I hate them, especially the brass ones with frilly shades and dangling light pulls that are supposed to look cottagey. I told Seth that fixed uplighters worked well in modern buildings with large windows and plenty of natural light, but they were not what were needed in the farmhouse. It had lots of dark nooks and crannies, so a mixture of standard and table lamps would be better. Light needed to be flexible and easy to move to where it was needed. Anglepoise lamps would be good in some places. I thought a successful design was going to be all about light.

I suddenly realised that I had been lecturing my mentor, and came to a stop. Seth looked at Joyce and they both began to grin.

"For goodness' sake, tell him, Seth."

I looked at them both, wondering what was coming next.

"We've both looked at your sketches and ideas and I must admit, Peter, you have the bones of a good design here. We especially liked your emphasis on light. It would have been easy to be lazy and go for fashionable fixed uplighters, but it would have made no sense. I'll put this to the client.

"On another matter, we've had two more recommendations come in off the back of the work we did at the Tudor house. Two more designs to complete. One is a conversion of an old warehouse. It's only a small job, but one where your study of modern design will be useful. I will go through everything with you before it goes to the client, but basically the job will be yours. You will have to work alongside the client's architect. If we get the contract, we'll talk about a bonus and where the future might be for us working together."

Joyce asked how Dougie was settling in. I told her about his accident and how everyone is nervous on their first day up the scaffold. I also mentioned that John and Cliff had adopted him and that with their support he couldn't fail. She smiled.

We were about to leave when I remembered my promise to Hannah's nan. I explained to Seth and Joyce that I was sort of going out with the girl next door to his Crescent project, and the girl's grandmother, who owned the place, would like to meet him, as they were to be neighbours. Seth laughed and Joyce smiled.

"You're telling us you are going out with Lady Roxford's granddaughter?"

I told them, sort of, but it would be nice if I could arrange for them to meet Hannah's nan.

Seth looked at me. "For God's sake, Peter, do you know what you're getting into?"

The answer was no, I didn't, but I wasn't going to admit anything. He looked at me, saying, "You are a constant surprise, Peter, but this is something else. Maybe the only thing that could beat it would be you walking in here one day with a decent beard."

*

Seth's question played on my mind. On my Wednesday visit to the Central Library, I looked up the Roxford family. Nothing about the family's past gave me any clues as to where Hannah and her grandmother were now. They obviously weren't as wealthy as the family had been, but their current position was hidden from public view. Why piss about, I thought, I'd ask her the next time we were alone together.

The next time we were to meet was on the Saturday and if that wasn't going to be a good time, then when was. Hannah told me her nana had some family visiting and she wanted Hannah and me to be at the meal arranged for that evening. Could we meet in the afternoon for a walk on Clifton Downs?

We met by the Observatory, not far from Brunel's legendary bridge.

She looked really nervous, even more so when I asked what was happening.

"They're a bunch of swine, Peter, the ones Nana has spent good money on to fetch in caterers. They just want to know how close Nana is to leaving this world and how they will benefit. I am the only thing that stands between them and Nana's money."

"You've not exactly found the right person to scare them away."

"I'm not sure of that. Nana thinks you won't be what they're expecting and will throw them off track. They'd know how to get to one of their own. It's her idea, not mine."

I told her I'd play the part, but we'd need to talk.

"What am I supposed to be to you: friend, boyfriend, minder?"

"Would it be so hard to be my boyfriend?"

"What would Lady Roxford think of that? You and a penniless working-class lad?"

"She likes you, Peter, and she is not a snob. The others who will be there are, and will look down their noses at you. They will do their best to make you feel out of place. They are Granddad's brother's offspring. Clara is his daughter. Their side of the family lost most of their money being who they are: feckless, self-entitled and stupid. They will fight to get hold of Nana's money and I wouldn't put anything past them. Clara and her husband Teddy will be there with their daughter Tamsin and the two sons, Craig and Jonathan. They wanted Jonathan and me to marry. No chance of that, as I strongly suspect Jonathan has no appetite for women, but that wouldn't stop them trying. I really don't know what the evening will bring, but I'd like you by my side at all times. Peter, I really need you to do this."

'Do you know what you're getting into?' Those words of Seth's were haunting me now.

I told her I had a lot going on in my own life at the moment, but I wouldn't let her down. As we walked back towards the Crescent she actually caught hold of my hand. That was a first, and one that scared me a little.

Drinks were being served in the sitting room. It would be half an hour before dinner was served in the room next door so I had a chance to observe the other guests. I was not very confident when I walked in, but the feeling only lasted for a few moments. They were like caricatures of the faded aristocrats I'd read about in Aldus Huxley's early novels. Hannah was a modern woman, so I couldn't see what there was to fear at first, but I soon sensed a malign undercurrent. The difference between them and me was that they had a heavy investment in the evening's proceedings. I, on the other hand, couldn't have given a shit. They would find their snobbery was something that could be turned against them. I actually began to welcome the coming conversation over dinner.

Hannah never left my side and, when her grandmother stood to lead everyone to the dining room, she called Hannah and me to stand beside her. I could see the worry on Clara and Teddy's faces. Hannah's hand never left mine as I assisted the old girl to the head of the dining table in the room next door and pulled out her chair for her. Hannah was next to her grandmother, with me on her other side, so she was effectively cut off from the rest of them. I quickly decided that Clara was enemy number one. Next to me going down the table was the female cousin, Tamsin, then Craig. Teddy and Jonathan were next to Clara on the opposite side. The table was one that could be extended by a winding mechanism. It had been made big enough for everyone to be comfortable, but small enough for everyone to hear what was being said.

The caterers served the first course, a sort of upside-down onion tart which Hannah later told me was a Shallot Tatin. I wasn't daunted by the amount of cutlery; I just watched what the others did.

As the dishes from the first course were being cleared away, Clara started with the inevitable questions. I made my answers as short as possible. What did I do? I worked in design, and so on. Questions about my family were met with vague answers. I wanted to tell her to stick her nose somewhere else, but I could see Lady Roxford was watching me closely.

The guy serving the wine kept approaching me to see if my glass needed refilling. It didn't and wasn't going to be. Tamsin wanted to know if the design company I worked for was one she would know. I told her no, as we worked only in Bristol and strictly by recommendation for a limited number of clients. She was knocking back the wine as if it was about to become as scarce as water was in some desert somewhere. By the time the second course came, I could see Tamsin was losing any inhibitions she might have had. Jonathan was saying nothing, but looking me over as if I was a potential bed mate. Craig seemed totally disinterested, but was as keen as his sister on the red wine.

I could sense there were two questions they desperately wanted to ask. How long had I known Hannah, and what was she to me? I wasn't going to volunteer the answers so, unless one of them was brave enough to ask, they'd be left hanging.

Eventually, Clara asked Hannah where we'd met. Hannah gave an inventive, though fabricated, answer.

"Oh, I'd gone to a party with this guy. He seemed bright, but as the evening wore on he only talked about his work. A science graduate from Cambridge, if I remember correctly. He never asked about me, so I decided I'd look for someone who would. Peter looked as if he was bored with the whole thing and sensed I was, so after a long conversation we left together."

Tamsin wanted to know what happened next. Hannah just gave her a dismissive look.

"I can't stand safe men," said Tamsin. "I like my men to be a little risky, a little dangerous."

I asked what she meant by risky, but didn't give her a chance to answer.

"For me," I said, "risky men are those with a little charisma who can talk people into doing things they would never do if they stopped to think about it. The risk is never theirs. They treat women with disrespect, talk men into gangs or uniforms, while all the time they keep themselves safe with some excuse or another. They are deceitful, and that is the one quality I cannot stand in either man or woman. I like my men and women to be honest and to do what they say they are going to do."

I couldn't see what Lady Roxford was doing behind the hanky she was holding to her mouth, but I could see that Hannah was desperately trying to keep a straight face.

That was my only contribution to the conversation. It seemed I'd told them all they needed to know.

The evening stuttered along after that with Tamsin and Craig hitting the wine pretty hard. Clara remained calm but it was clear she wasn't happy. When it was time to go, Hannah and I followed them into the hallway to collect their coats and see them out to the waiting taxis. I was asked if I could be dropped off somewhere. Hannah told them no, as I wasn't leaving. Clara's face was a picture.

The house had gone back to quiet and I asked Hannah, what now? "Let's go and see Nana," she said. We found Nana in a cosy little room behind where we'd eaten. Sitting with her was the old man from upstairs.

"Thank you, Peter; my goodness, you are a breath of fresh air. You managed to leave no doubt in their minds that you knew what they were up to without spelling it out. You are a clever man."

I didn't think so, but realised that sometimes just being honest can do the job.

The old man stirred in his chair. "I heard it all; couldn't imagine their faces but felt their discomfort through the wall."

"Peter, this is Carl, my companion. He'll deny it, of course, as he is a stickler for keeping up appearances. However, I'd be lost without him."

I realised that exposing her relationship with her driver was a show of trust in me. She insisted I drop the Lady Roxford and call her Esmé. I wanted to know more about Clara and her family. Esmé obliged.

"My husband's brother, George, was a lot younger than him. An accident, it was rumoured, as his mother was not keen on another child after a difficult birth with Reg. She'd found it hard to conceive, so when she fell pregnant it wasn't expected. Ten years makes a big difference. Reg felt that he was more like an uncle to George than a brother. George never had the economic sense my husband Reginald had. Reg told me that he had his doubts about the unprecedented rise in share prices in the 1920s. The whole thing was unsustainable in his eyes. Reg began to shift from shares into property from 1923.

"No one was immune from the consequences of the crash, but his brother George wouldn't take advice. When the crash came, they lost heavily. George sank into depression and, straight after a meeting with his brokers, walked in front of a bus. After his death, the true extent of his debts were discovered and his wife Elizabeth found herself without any money and pregnant with Clara. My husband felt that he should have done more to help George. I told him he shouldn't feel guilty. However, he was not going to see Elizabeth suffer, and sold up some of his property to set up a trust fund to provide for Elizabeth and Clara. When Elizabeth died, the trust fund continued to support Clara. All except Jonathan have lived off its income ever since.

"I am of the opinion that it has done them no good. I became head trustee when Reg died. I've been trying to change the rules of the Trust so that if Tamsin, Jonathan or Craig have children it will only provide for their education and the education of future generations. They don't know about this yet. Providing them with an income has clearly not helped. They are worried because I am getting old and Hannah will take my place as Head Trustee when I die. Apart from Hannah, they are my only living relatives. If anything happens to Hannah, they will inherit."

I thanked Esmé for being so open and honest with me. She just smiled and said that if anyone was owed thanks it might be me.

Hannah complained she was feeling tired after dealing with the visitors. Esmé laughed and said she would see us tomorrow. Hannah caught my hand and we left for the basement.

"My God, Peter I need a drink."

"You and me both. What is it with your cousins. Have they never bloody worked?"

"No, I can't say they all have. Johnny has, and he's okay, but obviously hiding his sexual preferences. I'd have liked to have known him better, but Clara's ambitions for us stood in the way. Tamsin is a self-obsessed fool, but Craig really worries me. There is something malign about him; something bad."

"Can we change the subject now?" I said, "I have some good news. Well, good for me, anyway."

I told her about my design and Seth wanting me to do a complete project. She seemed excited for me and asked if she could look at it before I gave it to Seth.

She went off into the kitchen and reappeared with a bottle of Rioja and two glasses. There was more talk about work and family. It seemed that I wouldn't be ushered into a taxi that night. She told me the bed was made up in the spare room.

Not long after I had closed my eyes, I felt someone raise the sheets and climb in beside me. We clung to each other like crazed fools before the inevitable happened. I was awake when the dawn light began to dispel the darkness. She had her back to me, but must have heard me move. Turning to face me, she looked at me with tired eyes and asked, "We did alright, didn't we?"

"For a pair of beginners, you mean?'

"How did you know?"

"The same way you did, I guess. They say practice makes perfect, but we seem to have a pleasant overload of lust at the moment."

Hannah laughed. "Are you suggesting we should engage in more practice?"

Chapter 9

I didn't get back home until the Monday evening and, when I did, Jenny told me that Natalie had been on the phone and was really upset. Could I ring her? I didn't feel I owed her anything, but she was the caring sort, so something bad must have happened for her to ring me.

It was Leon. He had set up a workshop with a mate and bought in some second-hand machinery. One of the bits of kit was a spindle moulder. I knew these to be one of the most dangerous of the joiners' tools. The design was basically a series of cutting blades bolted down onto a spindle. Arrangement of the cutter blades determined the shape that would be moulded along the edge of the wood. It was used for everything from architraves to large picture frames.

At a thousand rpm, the equivalent of one hundred and thirty miles an hour, if a cutter comes loose or breaks, the bloody things can do serious damage. Leon had a piece of one in his chest and was in Frenchay Hospital. I decided I'd go visit.

Frenchay Hospital had housed American troops during the war. It was a series of long corridors with wards that were once dormitories on each side. Leon was in a serious injuries unit propped up on large pillows. He looked at me and I could see he needed to get something off his chest as well as the piece of metal out of it. I decided to tell it as I meant it then rather than as I would have said it when I first heard of him getting together with Natalie.

"No bad feelings, mate. How the shit did you end up here?"

"I should have checked the cutters more closely as I put them on the moulder."

"Bad luck."

"Negligence, the insurance company will call it."

"Sometimes I wonder why we bother paying the bloody parasites. What do the medics say?"

"I'll have one damaged lung. No more joinery for me: the dust would be lethal. Seven years out of my life building a future. One mistake. Life stinks sometimes."

"What does Natalie say?"

"What do you think? I've told her to walk away, but she won't. She says I can do other things and she'll work with me to do them."

"She's a pretty strong woman."

"Yes, I feel bad for taking her from you."

"You didn't, Leon. She chose you. Anyway, I've found someone else. I'm cool."

I left feeling more worried about him than I thought I might have been. I rang Natalie when I got home to let her know his spirits were good, if not as high as she'd have liked them.

I got a call from Hannah on the Tuesday to ask if I was coming on Wednesday evening. Frankly, I couldn't wait. Apparently, Esmé wanted us to have dinner with Carl and her. Hannah was going to cook.

Seth had been on site on Monday to see how close to finishing we were. He explained to John and Cliff that we had some projects in the pipeline, but for now he needed them on a new-build contract. Dougie would learn a lot working with them on a big site. I was to go back to Royal York Crescent. He'd let me know when the architect had finished the drawings for the small warehouse conversion and I would be given time to work on them. I asked again about a meeting with Lady Roxford. He told me to arrange something when I was back working there and he and Joyce would fit in with what I'd planned.

As I walked up Park Street towards Clifton on the Wednesday evening, I began to think about Esmé's motives for the dinner/supper invitation. That I was in a relationship with Hannah was obvious, but I wasn't a smart-arse graduate, son of a business family, or piece of aristocracy, or anyone else that might be considered suitable for a Lady's granddaughter. I'd known Hannah for a while now and she certainly knew what she was taking on. I was sure money was the big worry and that was the motive for dinner. I was sort of right, but sort of wrong when it came to it.

Melissa was sitting out on the steps as I passed. She called out, "Hey, your boss is going to make my friends homeless." I asked what she meant. She told me the students on the first floor wouldn't be allowed back next year. I said I couldn't spare them much sympathy; my tax was paying towards their education and I was sure their mummies and daddies wouldn't let them end up on the streets.

"You're a nasty, cynical man," she told me. "Anyway, how's it going with basement woman? Rumour is, she has royal blood."

I smiled. I had seen a spot of Hannah's blood, and it was definitely not blue.

"Where on earth did that story come from?"

"Can't reveal my sources," said a grinning Melissa, as she walked up the steps into Seth's place.

Hannah met me at the door and we went down into the basement. She was in the middle of cooking, but seemed relaxed. When she'd finished stirring the sauce and spreading it over the contents of a baking dish, she gave her full attention to me.

"Nana's going to ask lots of questions. She's just being protective. I'm trying not to be, but I'm more nervous now than when you met Clara and the cousins."

When the food was ready, she tugged on a bell pull in the corner then went to something that looked like a small lift which she called a dumbwaiter. She put the food inside, pressed a button and it disappeared to the floor above.

We walked into the dining room to find the table set for four and Carl bringing the food over. We talked intermittently through the meal, but the serious questions didn't come until after we'd eaten and Carl had brought coffee. It was then Esmé asked me how I saw my future.

I asked what she meant – my possible future with Hannah, my ambitions as an interior designer, my hopes to create my own business?

"You say your possible future with Hannah. Aren't you sure of your feelings for her?"

I looked at, Hannah, whose face was giving nothing away.

"Esmé, I don't command the words that would leave you in no doubt about how I feel for Hannah. We have known each other for a while, but somehow we have only now come to realise the strength of our feelings for each other. We have a lot more to discover. Frankly, I can't believe what has happened and I worry that Hannah will wake up one morning and decide she's made a big mistake.

"Hopefully, we will build a modern relationship where we are equal partners, which means that the question of our future is one for Hannah just as much as it is for me. It must worry you that I might try taking advantage of Hannah. If so, you underestimate your granddaughter. She is the brightest woman I have ever met.

"With regard to my ambitions as an interior designer, Hannah has offered advice, but I want the business to be one that I will build on my own. The other avenue might be a partnership with Seth and Joyce. I am already working on my first design for a warehouse conversion for them. Which reminds me, Seth and Joyce would like us all to go out for lunch one day soon. Now, what I would like to know is how does Hannah see her future?"

Hannah turned to face her grandmother. "Now, do you see why I feel as I do, Nana?"

Carl was grinning from ear to ear. "She should do, because Peter is just like your nana when she met her husband."

"Stop it, Carl."

"No, Esmé. Your nana had her own ideas about her future and wanted to be independent. A lot of compromises were made before she accepted him. If Hannah is a strong woman, she gets it from her grandmother. You two will find your way; I'm sure of it."

"Thank you, Carl, but I'm supposed to be the judge here. Peter, I like you, and I hope you and Hannah do find your way. She's told me how she feels about you."

"Nana, don't you dare tell him!"

"I see. So, despite you being a modern woman, you still wish to maintain some of our old ways? Feminine wiles are not beyond you."

"Certainly not; how do you think he ended up here?"

The two women burst into laughter. Carl just looked at me and rolled his eyes.

*

Later, when we were on our own in the basement, I told Hannah that from the following Monday I would be working next door for a few weeks. She suggested I bring some clothes and stay with her while I was working there. That way, she told me, I can find out if you're the kind of guy who leaves his clothes all over the place and somehow expects them to be washed, ironed and magically put away by the house fairy. I told her not to worry – her washing machine was the same as the one at home, and my sisters had never let me get away without doing the same chores they were expected to do. I am a fully domesticated male, I told her. I also mentioned what I thought might happen if Melissa saw a pair of my underpants hanging on the garden line. She laughed, saying, "Smalls go over the drier next to the AGA."

The last few days at the Tudor house went by quickly. John and Cliff were good company and it was going to be much quieter working on my own. The scaffold was down now and the final touches and snagging were under way. Seth called in on the Thursday with the architect's plans and sketches for the small warehouse conversion. He wanted me to go with him on the Saturday to look at the building before work started, just so I could get a sense of the space involved.

Kate, the owner of the Tudor house, became quite emotional on the Friday when it was time for us to say goodbye. She'd given us all a small brown envelope and told us we were always welcome to call in during the week if we were passing. As I said before, she was about as good a client as you could get.

*

Saturday evening I told Mum I would be staying at Hannah's while I was working at Royal York Crescent. She wasn't unduly surprised as I had been spending quite a few nights away from home. However, she wanted to know all about Hannah and why I'd never brought her home. I told her everything I knew and said I would bring her to meet everyone soon. I neglected to mention the Lady Roxford bit, as I knew this might fluster her needlessly. My sisters were just as inquisitive, Caroline especially, as she had her eyes on my room. Sally had formed a negative opinion of Hannah, which she was trying to shake off. Jenny seemed the least interested. I felt there had been something on her mind for a while. As it turned out, I only had to wait a day to find out.

*

I arrived at Hannah's, complete with rucksack, late on Sunday morning. There was a strong aroma of roast pork coming up from the basement. She told me she had prepared a Sunday lunch for us all so we could have the day free. I didn't mind; Hannah's cooking was something else, most likely because she took a strong interest in it and enjoyed doing it so much.

She was to be in Oxford on Wednesday so would travel up Tuesday afternoon, but be back by early Wednesday evening. She asked if I'd like to cook. I told her I'd book a table at El Roble. She laughed, but didn't object this time. Dinner with Esmé and Carl went well, with a pleasing lack of the tension that had featured the last time we ate together. I helped clear up and suggested we take a walk to burn off some of the calories we'd consumed. She thought a walk in the fresh air was a good idea, so we headed for the Observatory and then up onto the Downs.

Sometimes, when you're deep in conversation, you miss what's going on around you. It was like that for us at the time. I hadn't noticed the two women walking in front of us and I don't think Hannah had until one of them raised her voice.

"Why won't you let us tell everyone? Am I that embarrassing, or are you just too afraid to admit what you are, Jenny? I can't go on like this."

I turned to Hannah and put a finger to my lips, indicating we wait and listen. She shook her head and made to move on. I whispered, "Wait, this is important; trust me." She raised her eyebrows questioningly.

"I'm sorry, but I just don't know how to tell my family and the people we work with; you know what they're like. It's too hard."

I couldn't leave it any longer and called out to my sister.

"Hi, Jenny."

She turned quickly, looking alarmed, and asked how much I'd heard. I told her everything and not to freak out about it, but to introduce us to her friend.

Jenny turned to her partner then back to me. "This is Debbie, the woman I love. Debbie, this is my brother Peter."

I held out my hand to Debbie. "Pleased to meet you, Debbie. This is Hannah, the woman I love."

Hannah was trying to be serious but I could see a grin breaking through.

"I'm sorry, you two, we seem to have interrupted something. We can leave you to it or you can come for a coffee at my place. I have been waiting to meet one of the sisters Peter has told me so much about."

Jenny looked unsure but Debbie held out her hand and Jenny took it. The end of a quiet stroll across the Downs.

After we reached Hannah's apartment, she vanished to make tea. I knew what she was doing and took the opportunity she had given me. Jenny and Debbie sat opposite me on one of the sofas, still holding hands and seemingly reluctant to let go.

"Okay," I said, "let's get this out of the way. Jenny, I've noticed how unhappy you've been at home and I wish you had spoken to me about it. I'm really glad you've found someone you love and who loves you. As for the rest of the family, it's your story and you must tell it how and when you will. I'll not be saying anything."

Hannah chose this moment to return with tea and biscuits. She turned to Debbie, asking if she hadn't seen her recently at an exhibition of Giacometti's drawings for his well-known sculptures. Debbie said she'd been there and asked if she could take a closer look at Hannah's paintings. Hannah stood with her and led her back to the top of the stairs, explaining about each picture as they came down. Hannah said that most of the paintings had been her father's but she had added to the collection. She had even painted one or two of them herself.

"Peter, Hannah is..."

"Yes, I know, Jenny; Debbie is quite something too."

"Can we meet somewhere, just the two of us? I really need to talk to someone."

"Can you come after work to the Spanish restaurant on Park Street about half six on Tuesday? Hannah will be in Oxford that evening. It's called El Roble. Just so you know, everything we say I'll be telling Hannah."

"That's what lovers do, I guess. She seems nice and seems to understand."

Hannah was at the bottom of the stairs, standing in front of a picture with Debbie. It was one I'd noticed on my first visit. A portrait in black and white of a young girl looking very lonely and very sad. Debbie asked if it was a self portrait by Hannah. I didn't need to ask; I knew. It couldn't be anyone else or by anyone else.

*

"I see you've moved in next door."

Fag-rolling Melissa had caught me drinking tea on the steps outside.

"Just lodging there while I'm working here."

"God, Peter, most men would be shouting it from the roof tops if they were sharing space with basement woman. You're a bloody mystery."

"I like that; let's keep it that way."

I asked her about the guy from the party, and she told me that was another story. For once, she didn't have that confident smile that usually occupied her face. I didn't pursue it, thinking she must have friends she could share her troubles with. I was wrong.

*

Jenny was waiting outside when I arrived at El Roble on the Tuesday evening. I'd never seen one of my big sisters as unsure of themselves as Jenny appeared to be.

"Debbie is insisting she join us for drinks at The Greyhound later. She wanted to come with me, but I put my foot down."

When we entered, the waiter, Jorge, greeted us and showed us to the table by the window that I'd so often shared with Natalie. I introduced Jenny to him, explaining that she was my sister. He smiled and went to fetch the menus.

I knew Jenny needed to feel at ease, so I ordered a bottle of wine that I knew Hannah favoured and told her to try a glass. She gulped it down and then looked around the restaurant to make sure no one was in earshot. I poured her another glass, which she made short work of. It made her brave enough to say, "I'm queer, Peter. Your sister is a queer, a lesbo, a dyke. I love her, Peter. What the hell am I supposed to do?"

"What do you want to do?"

"I don't know. I'd just like us to live quietly together somewhere. Debbie does nothing quietly; she wants the world to know. The world's not ready and I don't want to be a bloody martyr for the lesbian cause."

I told her I understood, but I didn't completely. We ate and then made our way to The Greyhound. It was the place where the Beats and Folkies met, including those who occupied the bridge end of Royal York Crescent. Debbie was sitting alone at a small table.

"You decided to come, then?"

Debbie was halfway to being pissed. This wasn't going to be easy. I looked at them, told them they'd both drunk too much, so they could leave now and come home with me or I was off. They came. The spare room was unoccupied, as I'd moved into Hannah's bed. I made them coffee and told them how I saw it. Debbie wasn't pleased. She knew nothing of my sister and our working-class background. She was a graduate full of rebellion whose sexuality had become a cause. If she loved my sister she'd better try and understand the difficulties she faced. The mood seemed to grow sombre after that. We had coffee and went to bed. The next day, I would have to explain to Hannah about her uninvited guests.

*

Hannah called in to see me when she got back on Wednesday afternoon. I explained about the unmade bed. She told me not to worry – what else was I supposed to have done. She did say that it was odd having people coming into her flat when she wasn't there. It was her safe space, her comfortable hideaway. Then she laughed and reminded me of her wish for sisters. I reminded her of my comment about being careful what you wished for.

Jorge looked at me quizzically when I walked through the door of El Roble with Hannah on my arm. I introduced Hannah as my girlfriend. God only knows what was going through his head. Hannah was fascinated by the menu and when Jorge came to take our order she had lots of questions about the dishes and their ingredients. Jorge seemed pleased and suggested that if we liked fish we should try the merluza à la riojana: hake with tomatoes, peppers, onions, garlic, and paprika. We decided to try it. Hannah chose a bottle of Albariño and a tomato ensalada for us to start with. Hannah's fascination with food and knowledge of wine was beginning to rub off on me.

"Debbie doesn't get Jenny's situation."

I was trying to explain why it wasn't easy for Jenny to come out. Debbie is a casual where Jenny works; she will move on when the right opportunity occurs and will probably be in an environment where being gay is accepted. Working in the office of a construction company full of men... well, you can imagine what Jenny would face.

"I think Debbie's crusade is blinding her to the hurt she is going to cause Jenny if she forces her to come out. It's not just at work. My parents will struggle to understand and Sally, the eldest, well, she's as straight as you can be. Wait until you meet Graham. Sally will not like having a sister who's gay. She'll be worried that it will reflect on her. I don't think Caroline would care, and Mum and Dad love Jenny too much to let it become a problem. However, I know they would rather she kept her sexuality private. Debbie doesn't get any of this, or at least I don't think she does."

Hannah stayed silent, then reached for my hand. "I understand what you're saying. Nobody cared that much at university apart from a few cavemen. I've never really thought about what it would be like for people from a different social background. Can I meet your family soon?"

Well, she wouldn't have to wait long to meet Jenny again. She was sitting outside of Seth's project with Melissa, smoking a roll-up. Jenny didn't smoke, or at least I thought she didn't. It was out of character so I knew something was wrong.

Melissa smiled at me as we walked toward them.

"Your sister has been telling me all about you, Peter. Hannah, I'm jealous."

The smile had returned to Melissa's face. She turned to Jenny. "You alright now, girl?"

Jenny nodded.

"Then I'll see you tomorrow in The Greyhound?"

"Yes," said Jenny, "you will."

Jenny walked with us to the steps into Hannah's.

"I'm sorry to be a pain, Hannah, but can I talk with you and Peter for a while?"

It was only eight o'clock, so the evening was quite young. I knew there was a big unburdening coming and the unmade bed might not be remade that night. Hannah led the way down into her flat and I led Hannah into the kitchen.

"You okay with this?"

She pulled me toward her and gave me a full-on kiss in response.

I left her to the tea-making. Jenny sat quietly until Hannah came with a tray of tea mugs.

"Okay, tell us."

"I can't believe what I've done. I threatened to ditch Debbie if she persisted and she said she'd out us there and then. I told her to do it and I would leave and go find another job. She walked out. It's thanks to you, Peter. You made me realise how bloody selfish Debbie was being. It was a shock realising how strongly I felt for Debbie, but it was never going to work. Hannah, I'm sorry to burden you with all this."

Hannah just smiled and went to fetch three glasses and a bottle of her favoured red.

Jenny said she still cared for Debbie, but it had all been so tense. Debbie came to study here in Bristol and the women in the circle Debbie moved in were all radicals from her university days.

"I didn't really fit in. It was like I'd entered another world. I grew up thinking about how everyone around me would follow the age old path that Sally is following: courtship, engagement, marriage, then kids. It was something I knew I didn't want from the age of fifteen. To be honest, there are not many girls on our estate who would admit to having the feelings I have, and Debbie was the first girl I knew I could be open with. Now that I've ditched her, I should feel upset, but instead I feel liberated somehow."

"So, what's with the meet with Melissa?"

"She asked me out. I've got nothing else on so I'm going."

I explained how I felt about Melissa and how we liked to keep our business private. Jenny laughed and told us that from her brief conversation with Melissa she thought she might know more about me than I did, but she would respect our privacy.

I thought it wise to try and get the conversation going in a different direction so I told them about Leon. Hannah was visibly shocked and I thought I saw a tear. Jenny wanted to know how Natalie was taking it. I told her what Leon had told me. Hannah didn't respond, but Jenny thought Natalie must have been either deeply in love or unable to cope with the guilt if she walked away. I explained that I thought it was the former. Hannah said she'd ring Natalie soon. Jenny apologised to Hannah once more for burdening us with her problems. Hannah gave her a hug in reply. Burden us with them or not, it was eleven before we found our beds.

*

The following evening when I got back from work, interesting aromas were coming up from the basement. Hannah greeted me with a kiss and told me to go get washed and changed. I wasn't daft and knew this was leading up to something. When I reappeared, a glass of wine was put in my hand and I was told to sit.

"Your sisters made me think."

"How?"

"Did you share your sister's expectations when you were fifteen?"

"You mean: love, courtship, marriage, and all that? To be honest, I never thought about it. I sort of pushed thoughts of it into the future somehow. After Seth started taking my work seriously and began mentoring me, work occupied a lot of my thinking."

"So, how do you see our relationship developing?"

"That's not entirely down to me, but I'm not bothered about marriage, although I would like kids at some stage."

She walked across to the sofa, pushed me backwards while giving me a big hard kiss on the mouth. "I love you, Peter; you seem to know exactly what to say. Now let's eat."

CHAPTER 10

Seth turned up at the Crescent on Wednesday. He told me another two weeks and I was to act as site manager at the farmhouse job. I was effectively in charge and would have to deal with the builder and scaffolder. Seth would be on hand as project manager. He asked if I was ready for this. "Now or never," I told him. He gave me the architect's plans for the warehouse conversion and told me not to be disappointed if he made major revisions; I should get my final scheme in within fourteen days. He told me that a certain woman had indicated I had moved in with Lady Roxford's granddaughter. I forgave Melissa as I knew it would be general knowledge soon anyway. I promised to organise a lunch with Lady Roxford before the farmhouse project started.

*

It was Hannah who raised it. Two weeks had gone by and I was due to start at the farmhouse in Westbury-on-Trym on the Tuesday. I'd arranged for Seth and Joyce to come to lunch on the Monday and Hannah said she'd do some salads and things.

"Nana wants to know if I'm moving you in permanently and if so how much rent I'm going to charge you."

"And are you?"

"Am I what?"

"Going to move me in permanently?"

"I thought you'd worked that one out."

"We'll go visit my lot on Sunday. I'll need to pick up some stuff. I'm pretty sure Jenny would have told them all about you and who your grandmother is. Mum will be flustered, but don't expect my sisters to curtsy. Caroline will be more than pleased to get a bedroom of her own. Sally will pretend to be totally unimpressed by your obvious beauty and Dad will sit in his chair waiting for us all to go and for things to settle down again. We are a pretty normal family, Hannah."

She asked me if every working-class family had a Peter and a Jenny. The answer was no, and I had to admit that the families on the estate were a mixed bunch. She said I would benefit from reading a little sociology. "Put the books on the pile marked 'must read'," I told her, "and I'll get round to it sometime."

I rang Mum straight away and we got an invite to Sunday lunch. Mum's Sunday lunch was about as good as you could get, so no criticism from my cooking-obsessed girlfriend was on the horizon. Not that she would have said anything anyway.

*

It was Friday, and the bell rang just as Hannah was cooking dinner. It was Jenny with Melissa in tow. She could see I didn't look best pleased and just told me to be cool. I told her we would be eating soon, but this didn't put her off. It was Melissa who asked if they could speak to us both. I called Hannah, who crossed the room and hugged them both. If there is such a thing as extrasensory perception then I am sure it only exists between certain females.

"I wanted to warn you both that Melissa is coming with me on Sunday and I am going to tell Mum tomorrow that I'm a lesbian."

I told Jenny it looked like it was going to be a fun Sunday lunch and asked if Graham was coming. He was working away, which was probably for the best. Hannah said it would be fine and asked if they would like to stay for dinner. She had cooked enough for four as she'd planned to freeze some. Melissa's grin would have illuminated the darkest cave. I realized that family is unshakeable, and thanked God that, while mine might be inconvenient sometimes, they could always be relied upon.

After we'd eaten and talked for a while about the family's possible reactions to Jenny's announcement, they asked if we would like to go to The Greyhound with them. Hannah begged off, saying she was tired and needed an early night. I just smiled and told Hannah an early night would be good. Melissa grinned, but didn't comment. I could guess what was going through her mind.

When they were gone, I told Hannah to work out what she paid weekly for gas, electricity and so on and I'd pay half. It was important I pay my share. She told me she didn't pay rent as the house was effectively hers. I could help with the bills, though, if I wanted to. I insisted. She said she'd let me know.

We sat quietly for a while and then I asked her about the thing that had been puzzling me for so long. "That day on the stairs when you asked me to go with you to the party – what made you do it?"

"To be honest, I'm not sure. You looked handsome enough, in a boyish sort of way, but I wasn't out looking for a boyfriend. I just wanted to move around without suffering the fate of some of the attractive girls I'd met at university. Men wanted to treat them like playthings, not real people. They were all on hormonal overdrive. One girl used to wear a badge saying, 'Would you lie to me, just to get inside of my pants?' I saw a lot of men doing it – stop smiling, Peter, you know I mean lying. Okay, I know I have hormones too, but I just didn't want to play that sort of game. I didn't want to be hunted, seduced and conquered. It's horrible to think about it now, but since we've met I've been using you as a barrier. You were right to say I'd become a bit paranoid. You didn't seem to care, just wanted to help. I couldn't work out why you weren't like all the other men. You actually treat me like I'm a human being.

"When I began to fancy you, you didn't seem that interested in me. The night you admitted you did changed everything. I was thrown into a panic. The next day I went to Nana and told her how I felt. She laughed, and told me it was time I started trusting myself. So, why did it take you so long to develop feelings for me?"

"As a man, there are some women you can only be friendly with or love like a mother or sister, and then there are some women who look and sound like you – women from a different social class: educated and, in your case, impossibly elegant. What are the chances that someone like you would fall for a guy like me? So, you get put in the unattainable box and life goes on. When I knew the box wouldn't hold you any more, I had to tell you. It's sort of comforting to know you'd been trying to break out of that box, because I was really wishing you would. Until that happened, I was quite happy playing along.

"I must admit, that when we went out together, I took pleasure in watching the men's faces when they realised you were with me. Even more so when they heard my accent and guessed my origins. It was quite an adventure helping you out, and I learnt a lot. I never thought for one moment I was being used in a bad way. I was always curious as to where you'd take me next."

"Peter, if your family are anywhere near like you, I can't wait to meet them."

I knew it would have to happen, but couldn't say I was joyous about it.

*

Hannah took ages getting ready on the Sunday morning and I was doing my best to stay cool. She'd told me she wasn't going to rush and she'd booked a taxi for half eleven. I had the final plans for the warehouse project spread out in front of me. Hannah had looked at them and made some good points. I'd give them to Seth on Monday – he'd suggested I take the day off before starting at the farmhouse on Tuesday. The taxi arrived on time, as did Hannah. What had taken her all that time to be any more elegant than she had been two hours ago I wasn't sure. I have since discovered that men are a bit dull when it comes to these sorts of things.

I'd told Hannah that it wasn't our custom to hug people on first meeting, but when Mum answered the door, complete with pinny, that was exactly what Hannah did. Then she told her the aromas coming from the kitchen smelt delicious and asked if she could help with preparing the meal. I could see Mum wasn't quite sure what to do, so she just led Hannah into the place she'd always kept the rest of us out of.

I went into the sitting room to find Dad sitting on his own in his usual chair. He told me my sisters were upstairs getting ready and Jenny, who hadn't come home last night, would be arriving with her friend shortly. He asked what I thought about Jenny saying she was a lesbian. I told him that if she was happy that way we should all be happy for her. He smiled. "Can't say I really understand it, but she's our Jenny and, as you say, we all want her happy." I knew there was something amiss so asked how Sally was taking it. He looked a little sad and told me Sally would get used to it. It would take a while, but it seemed Jenny was looking for a flat with her new friend. So a little separation might be good.

At that point, we heard laughter coming from the little kitchen next door and Hannah and Mum walked in wearing big smiles.

"Okay, Mum, what have you told her about me?"

Hannah turned to Mum, putting a finger to her lips. They were both happy, so I knew all was well. Hannah went across to Dad and, as he stood, she surprised him with a hug.

The table had been laid in the front room. It was a makeshift affair, with chairs brought from all over the house. The table was just about big enough for seven.

Caroline appeared from upstairs first and seemed surprised when she set eyes on Hannah. Hannah offered a hug and Caroline took it. When Sally came down, a frost flowed before her on the stairs. First a gay sister and now a woman she thought she must dislike. Hannah didn't offer a hug, just a hand, and said she was pleased to meet her. Sally took it without enthusiasm.

Just moments later the door opened and Jenny and Melissa walked in. Sally's face became stony, but their happiness seemed infectious. Hannah hugged them both, which encouraged Mum and Caroline to do the same. Sally disappeared into the kitchen and I followed her in.

"Tell me, Sally, did I treat Graham like you're treating Hannah and Melissa?"

"I don't want to talk, Peter. Don't worry, I won't upset the apple cart. I just want this dinner over and done with."

I was trying desperately to keep my anger contained and told her that Jenny would tell her where I lived if she wanted to come and explain herself. Then left her to it.

The meal went quite well, despite Madame Sullen sitting at the other end of the table. Jenny and Melissa were hardly giving way; they were happy and bubbling over with it. Even Dad got caught up in their sense of fun. This was my dad, who, if there was such a thing as working-class stoicism, would have been one of its leading philosophers. Never buy anything you don't need, enjoy what you have, avoid borrowing, and don't waste time wishing for things you'll never be able to afford.

Before we left, I could see that Hannah and Mum had sought refuge in the kitchen for a few moments.

When I asked what had been said, Hannah suggested we leave it until we were at home. The taxi that arrived was big enough for four, so Jenny and Melissa came with us. Mum would be lumbered with explaining to the neighbours the reason for the rare appearance of a taxi in our street.

*

Hannah was up early on the Monday and busy preparing the so-called 'simple salads'. Apparently, a chicken had to be roasted first in time for the meat to be cool enough to make a chicken salad. Cold meats were lain on a plate and covered and placed in the fridge. Then a Greek salad was prepared with tomatoes, peppers and feta cheese. New potatoes from Cyprus were boiled to form the basis of a potato and spring onion salad. As I said, just 'simple salads'. I offered to help, but was told to keep out of the way and focus on my warehouse conversion plans.

Carl came down at around eleven thirty to see how things were going and to explain that he would help with the serving, but wouldn't join everyone at the table. I asked what Esmé thought about this, and Hannah interrupted, saying Carl was a stubborn old man and Nana would probably have insisted he join us. I took a chance and said that I was with Esmé on this one and if he didn't join us I would take it personally. I told him Seth and Joyce were not snobs and I would find it difficult to sit at the table if he wasn't there. He left, not saying anything.

I had gone over the warehouse plans so often I was seeing them in my sleep. I would be glad to pass them to Seth. He arrived promptly at midday with Joyce on his arm. It was interesting to see them dressed smartly as if to impress. I must admit that I'd made an effort. There was something about the old lady that made you want to. We gathered in the formal sitting room on the first floor. Esmé winked at me as she walked in on Carl's arm. I introduced Seth and Joyce, and when the pleasantries were over, Esmé focused her questions on Seth's intentions for his project. Hannah nodded to me as soon as it seemed polite and explained we needed to put the final touches to lunch. We left for the basement.

"Don't be offended, but Nana will want to ask Seth and Joyce about you."

"You never told me about your conversation with Mum."

"People who care for us can be over-protective sometimes. Sally had said some things about me just using you. I told your mother I'd made mistakes but I truly loved her son. Nana likes you, but she will want to know more about you."

When Hannah was ready, she sent me upstairs and rang the bell on the dumbwaiter. I made sure I was next to it and that Carl stayed in his seat. One by one, I took the salads to the table and, when all was settled, Hannah sent up the wine. A light, slightly bubbly wine from Portugal called Vinho Verde and a Valencian red that I had told Hannah Seth favoured.

I listened carefully to the conversation between Seth and Lady Roxford. Despite being encouraged to do so, Seth never dropped from the formal and I could see Carl's approval. They agreed that any investment in Royal York Terrace at this time would be a wise one.

Lunch ended with Esmé feeling she had a sympathetic developer next door, Seth that he had at least one neighbour he wouldn't alienate when building work was under way, and Hannah and me feeling another milestone had been passed.

Hannah and Carl started clearing the dinner stuff away and I showed Seth and Joyce out. I walked into the street with them and along to where they'd parked their car.

"You're living with Hannah permanently now, Peter?"

It was Joyce who asked, but I knew Seth was just as curious. I told them yes, and if they asked how I'd managed to win Hannah's affections I didn't have any answers. Joyce looked at me with a rather serious face.

"I watched her, Peter; her eyes hardly left you all the time we were there. Her grandmother asked Seth about you. Seth sounded quite paternal, bless him. He painted a picture of a quick-learning, determined young man with a bright future. Then she asked me what I thought and I told her you were charming. She laughed and told me you'd certainly charmed a few people under her roof. The old lady seems very fond of you, and told us you came to help the evening she fell. I don't know where Carl fits in, but he referred to you as Miss Hannah's dear friend."

All this time Seth was silent. When we neared the car, he turned and said, "Peter, I'm speechless. How the hell did you end up with Hannah? I'm not going to say the obvious about contacts and clients, because she might come to her senses and kick you out tomorrow."

"Thank you, Seth, but you're right – it's early days yet."

Joyce laughed. "Honestly, you men. I saw what I saw and if you feel for her the way I sensed she feels for you this could be a relationship that could last some while."

Seth thanked me for the introduction to Lady Roxford and promised he would look over the plans with Joyce that evening. He wished me good luck for the first day at the farmhouse.

CHAPTER 11

Early mornings never bothered me. When you work in the trades, lying in is just for Sundays. I arrived at the farmhouse at ten to eight and the client met me in her dressing gown. I apologised for being early, and she replied that she was always up at six but just took a little time to come to. I told her I'd wait for Seth and the team in the garden. She told me not to be silly and to wait in the kitchen while she showered and dressed.

The farmhouse job was an unusual one as there were no other professionals involved. The opening up of the kitchen window to form French casements was the only structural change, so we didn't need an architect, an expense the client's husband was keen to avoid. The only other mess would come from the sparks: they would need to cut channels in the plaster for wires and new sockets. The builders, sparks, and plumber were to meet us at ten to discuss timing. In the meantime, my little team of John, Cliff and Dougie would start stripping the horrendous floral patterned wallpaper from the dining room walls and start prepping the woodwork.

The builder Seth had found for this job was a guy called Gary. He'd arrived before the others and disliked me from the word go. All he could see was a boy about to tell him what to do. I wasn't going to get on my knees and explain that I was the guy who'd created the design and his only job was to knock a fucking hole in the wall big enough for the carpenters to come and fill with French doors. When

Seth arrived, he put him straight and told him future work would depend on my approval. He told Seth he wouldn't take instructions from me, so Seth told him to go.

Seth said he'd call Jeff, the builder we'd worked with on the Tudor house. He'd have to explain why he hadn't called him in the first place, but Jeff was no fool. He would do the work if he could and gain a few more brownie points from Seth and me. I told Seth that price wasn't everything and reliability was priceless. He told me I still had a lot to learn.

Not a good start, but one the client couldn't have witnessed from upstairs. After that, things went smoothly enough.

The client, Diane, had warmed to us after a few days and started to supply us with mugs of tea and biscuits every few hours. She was the one who approved the plans, and when she saw something she wasn't sure of she sought me for advice. Her bank manager husband seemed quite happy to let Diane make decisions when unexpected problems cropped up.

Most days, I ate my sandwiches with the others in whichever room we were working in. Occasionally, I left the farmhouse, crossed the road and followed the Trym Brook to the gates of the parish church. The graveyard was quiet and a place I could think things over without the chatter of the others. You have to be careful you don't get so caught up in the day-to-day of the job that you lose the big picture.

It was one of those days. I was lost in thought when I heard my name spoken by a voice I didn't recognise. I looked up from where I was sitting on the bench and saw Hannah's cousin Johnny standing in front of me.

"Sorry, Peter, you seemed miles away, but I couldn't let this opportunity pass. Do you mind if I sit down?"

I wasn't sure what was coming, but I told him to sit anyway. He explained that he felt awkward because he'd assumed that Hannah must have told me about his mother's crazy plans. Marriage between first cousins was a definite no-no, but there was no way he was going down that road anyway. He told me he had always liked Hannah and now she was with me it might be a good time to see if we could become friends.

I said I'd talk to Hannah about it. He gave me a card with his number on and told me a guy called Tim might answer the phone. Apparently, Tim was his new flatmate, but the big smile accompanying his name gave me other ideas. I asked where his flat was. He told me it was in a four-storey block next to the farmhouse.

When I got home that evening I told Hannah about my encounter with Johnny. She seemed quite pleased and asked if I'd mind if she invited them for supper. It was her flat, yet she'd asked my permission. She could have just told me what she was going to do. I was beginning to believe Joyce might be right. I reached for her hand, pulled her to me, and kissed her. She asked, "What was that for?" I told her.

Johnny had jumped at the chance to build a friendship with Hannah and me. They would be coming for supper on Saturday. My sister Jenny was the first woman I knew who was openly gay. She told me gay was now the word preferred by homosexuals to explain their sexual orientation. It wasn't a word that had caught on that widely outside of their community, but I guessed it would. Johnny wasn't the first gay male I knew of. There were a few gay kids at school who tried to ward off violence and bullying by being excessively camp and making themselves a joke. It didn't always work. Some men's fear of the love of other men make them act in the cruellest ways.

When Hannah was preparing a meal she became someone best left to get on with it. There was a small door at the back of the kitchen that led to a short, vaulted subterranean room. It was where Hannah kept her wine and where I was sent with specific instructions. Johnny and Tim were due in half an hour.

Tim sat next to me and Johnny next to Hannah. I could see Hannah was keen to catch up with Johnny, so I took on Tim. He was tall, with a slightly receding hairline. Large glasses rested on a slightly upturned nose. He spoke quietly and with an accent I couldn't place until he told me he was originally from Newcastle. I discovered he was a jazz fan and, what's more, played the trumpet. I was embarrassed. He'd played locally and I'd never heard him. We talked about Miles, Chet and Lee Morgan and I told him he must let us know when he next had a gig. I'd looked through Hannah's records and guessed we had a lot to learn about each other's musical preferences. Tim, being a jazz player, might be a good place to start to introduce Hannah to jazz. No doubt she'd want me to go to the opera, as her record collection seemed to indicate that was where her musical preference lay.

When they'd left and we'd cleared the kitchen, Hannah asked what I'd thought. It seemed to me that Johnny had got out from a crazy situation at home. Clara was controlling; maybe his siblings weren't quite so lucky or maybe they were just spineless. I liked Johnny, but wasn't sure if making him a friend wouldn't stir a pot best left unattended. I told her what I'd learnt about Tim and asked if she would go with me to see him play. She told me she loved going to see live music.

"Wasn't it a jazz musician who once said there is no bad music, just musicians who couldn't do it justice?"

I told her they were the words of Archie Shepp and I was amazed she knew of him. She told me never to judge a girl by her record collection.

*

Tim rang the following Tuesday, saying he had a gig with a band at the White Hart on Friday, not far from where I was working. It was a rhythm and blues band and he was playing in the horn section. He reckoned the band was worth hearing. Hannah was due back from Oxford in the afternoon; she was keen to go as long as we didn't stay too late.

*

Walking along the Crescent after work on Thursday, I found Melissa sitting on the step outside Seth's project.

"How's my sister?"

"Not good – Sally is being a pain. I told Jenny to move in with me, but she's nervous of your sister."

"Are you seeing her tonight?"

"Every bloody night, that's what's so frustrating."

"You are gay, aren't you, Melissa?"

"I wasn't sure until I met your sister."

"And now?"

"I asked her to move in, didn't I?"

"Not sure how I can help; Hannah's away tonight. Are you going to The Greyhound?"

"Not sure."

"Come down and see me, if Jenny is up to it."

"I'll mention it. Anyway, looks like you and basement girl are a couple. When is the big day?"

"It's gone, Melissa – the big day happened a while ago and it's got nothing to do with the church or the law."

"Peter, I'm sorry. I was about to say something stupid. I'll ask Jenny."

I was almost ready to go to bed when the doorbell rang. It was Jenny. She'd told Melissa she was going home, but instead came to me. She was tearful and tried to explain what was going on in her head. Did she love Melissa? She didn't know. I told her to be cool. Melissa was offering her love. Why shouldn't she take it. Was it Sally trying to make her deny who she was? Jenny said, "No, it's me."

"Oh, Jenny, if we all look too closely at what we're doing, where would the spontaneity be? We would overanalyse everything. Please just go next door and jump into bed with Melissa. It might not end well, but who knows?"

"Is that what you did with Hannah?"

"No, Jenny, Hannah jumped into bed with me."

Jenny left then, and left me guessing what she'd do next. I found out the following morning when I caught sight of her rushing down the street as I made my way to work.

When I got back to the flat on the Friday, Hannah was already at home. I could see she was really tired and suggested we miss the gig that night. She didn't protest, just asked if that would be alright. I rang Johnny and asked him to pass our apologies to Tim. Then I turned my attention to Hannah.

"What's wrong?"

She looked at me with a weak smile and began to explain about her studies, the deadlines she was facing, and how she felt she had dropped behind. She'd been up late the night before, writing, which was why she was so tired. More time and lots of evenings working were needed. Her nana had an office upstairs which she could use to work without distraction. Would I mind if she focused on her studies for the next few weeks?

I realised that I was something she hadn't planned for, and I wasn't going to get in the way of her finishing her MA. I told her this and that I would use the time to do some studying of my own. She wanted to cook. I told her there was an amazing fish and chip shop nearby and to try and stay awake until I returned.

*

The weeks at the farmhouse passed quickly and it was soon time for the scaffold to go up outside. Gavin arrived one Monday to see what was needed.

"How are you getting on with your new position, boy?"

"Doing my best, Gavin, for as you know, all our doubts are traitors."

"You've been reading the Bard, I see. Come on, show me what you want, Peter, and I'll tell you what you can have."

I don't know why it felt that important to me to have this grumpy, Shakespeare-loving, scaffold boss's approval but I was glad to have it. I asked him about Donny. He smiled, saying, "He's a good lad, that one. Another couple of years and he'll be educated enough to leave scaffolding behind. I'll miss him, but something told me his destiny lay elsewhere." I told him that if all bosses read Shakespeare the world might be a better place. He laughed and told me to get on with it as he had work to do.

After Hannah told me of her need for study time, we fell into a quiet routine. Before and during dinner, we would exchange detailed accounts of our days. Then we would separate, with Hannah going to the study upstairs and me to the kitchen table. I knew Jenny had moved in next door, so I caught her one day and told her Hannah was studying hard to complete her dissertation. She took the hint. I asked about the family. She said she'd never speak to Sally again. Mum and Dad were upset, and I should go and visit them soon. What can you do when your eldest sister, the one you always went to for advice, suddenly turns into a judgemental monster. I said I'd go soon.

I began to realise that when Hannah set her mind to something it would be done. I'd stepped right back and left her working every evening she was home. I told her it was time I visited my family and that I planned to go on Sunday. I knew from our nightly exchanges over dinner exactly where she was in her dissertation and told her to stay and work. She reluctantly agreed then asked that I tell my mother she'd followed her advice. I asked what advice, and a wicked smile lit up her face.

*

It was Sally who answered the door.

"Oh, it's you. Mum and Dad are round at the Lamb and Lark; they'll be back soon."

"Good, it was you I wanted to talk to."

"I suppose you're going to go on at me about the way I've been treating Jenny."

"I could do, but I'm not, and neither am I going to go on at you about your attitude towards Hannah. What I want to know is what happened to my big sister? The one I went to for advice. The one who looked out for me and stopped me making a prat of myself. The sister I loved and, despite everything, I still love."

I wasn't expecting what came next. It was tears, and lots of them. I held her and told her to tell me.

"I don't love him, Peter. I don't love Graham. I'm not sure I ever have. I was doing what all my friends were doing. Finding a steady man with 'good prospects', being sensible, planning to settle down, and now I don't know how to get out of it. Seeing you and Jenny so happy made me realise how I'd trapped myself. I've been a bitch because of it. Your turn, little brother; maybe it's your turn to give me advice."

"Tell him, Sally, before it's too late. Graham's a decent bloke, but I never thought you would end up with a guy like him. Look, Sally, I'm not going to criticise him, but you are so much brighter. Don't go on making yourself unhappy. Best let him go before it's too late."

"I've been wanting to, Peter, and I build myself up to doing it every time we meet. Then my courage drains away."

"He'll be sensing something, Sally, just as I did with Natalie. He'll know something's not right. Get it over with soon."

When her eyes had become dry, I tried to change the subject. I asked how Caroline was coping. She looked surprised.

"You mean you don't know that she's been out partying with Jenny and Melissa? Apparently, she has been on a few dates with some folk musician guy."

I told her I didn't know. Hannah was up to her eyes in her studies, and we'd been keeping everyone at arms' length so she wouldn't be distracted. I told Sally that when Hannah had finished her dissertation I wanted her to come and meet Hannah on her own ground.

"You'll see what makes me feel the way I do. I know what you're thinking, but she's no snob and you are duller than I thought if you can't work out the way we feel about each other."

"She must hate me, Peter."

"Hannah said she always wanted sisters; she's about to hit the reality of her wish. You'll understand when you really know her."

When Mum and Dad got back from the pub, they sensed that a peace had been made between us. Mum asked after Hannah and I mumbled something about Hannah having accepted her advice. She laughed out loud, leaving the rest of us none the wiser. Mum wanted to know what I thought about Caroline spending so much time in Clifton. I looked at Sally and then at Mum and told her Caroline was in good hands. Sally stayed quiet.

*

When I got back, I found Hannah cooking a casserole of pork and apple. The aromas coming from the kitchen were making me hungry, when two minutes before I was sure that I hadn't been. She was keen to know the details of my visit, but I told her it was her turn to report first. She was smiling.

"I've got it, Peter – I've developed a structure to hang my points on and the conclusions are in my head. Another month or so and I hope it will be done."

I was given an overview, and it seemed sound to me. Now it was my turn. Hannah listened intently as I told her about Sally and the trap she had built for herself.

"Sally was taking her misery out on us. While we were happy, she was miserable, and she came to resent us. I think she will let Graham down gently, but he will hurt and I'm not sure how you can soften a blow like that. Sally thinks you must hate her. I told her I believed you were bigger than that and you would understand. I hope you do. She's been a pain, but she's still my big sister and I'm not going to give up on her."

Hannah told me that it had taken a lot to ignore Sally's attitude toward her; now she knew the reasons, she would try to understand. I told her about Caroline spending time with Jenny and Melissa and dating a folk musician from the squat. She laughed and told me that Caroline was one woman who tradition was not going to drag down. I asked her how she felt now about having sisters. She told me she couldn't understand how she'd managed to live so long without the drama.

CHAPTER 12

I was at the library looking over a pile of books, trying to work out which ones to take home, when he approached me. He was slightly shorter than me and carrying a bit more weight. His head seemed to grow directly out of his shoulders. From his large round face two small brown eyes looked across at me. He was wearing a suit, and a tie hung loosely from the neck of his shirt. Not the stuff of female dreams, I thought, but then, who was I to say?

He introduced himself, saying his name was Gareth, and told me he had noticed my interest in architecture. He was an amateur historian with a particular interest in the architecture of our city. We talked for a while and he said he did occasional city tours for the Workers' Education Association. The walks were to introduce people to the history of the city through some of its buildings. He asked me where I lived and, when I told him, he became really animated. I could see he was ready to go off on one, so I told him I had a meal waiting I shouldn't be late for. He gave me a leaflet with a list of his upcoming guided tours. I said I'd try and get to one.

When I got back, Hannah was just beginning to stir rice into what she told me was a paella. There was news, but I'd need to wait until we'd eaten. Making a paella was an art, and she needed to concentrate. Her food was always served in small portions, which was just as well as it was difficult to resist. I noticed she never offered more than what had been first served. I didn't mind; I felt a lot better for eating less. At home, if I'd said I liked something, Mum would have just kept piling food on my plate.

Hannah told me her supervisor in Oxford had rung. She'd sent a progress report the previous week with a summary and an outline of her dissertation, and he'd suggested she go up in the morning for a meeting. I didn't mind, though I was curious about the need for her to go so soon. She didn't know, but promised she'd tell all when she got back. She'd return straight after the meeting. Tim had rung to say he was playing at the White Horse the following evening. Would I mind going on my own if she wasn't up to it? It turned out that Hannah knew of the guy, Gareth, who had approached me in the library. He was self-taught and extremely knowledgeable. If I decided to go on one of his tours, Hannah would come with me.

When Hannah returned the following afternoon, she was full of it. The 'it' being the fact that her supervisor had talked to his colleagues and they had agreed that her dissertation had the potential to be turned into a doctoral thesis. Did she want to go ahead? Her face told me she did and I think mine must have told her that I wanted her to.

It was decided we'd celebrate by going to the White Hart that evening to hear Tim play. It was a bad move. Sitting with Johnny were Tamsin and Craig. It was too late to turn around; Craig had seen us. Hannah pulled me close and whispered that I should not let them provoke me. I wasn't going to, but maybe Hannah was going to provoke them. When we entered the room, she laughed, held me close and gave me a full-on kiss. Pulling away, she led me to a small table with two chairs next to the bandstand and then turned and casually waved at her cousins

The band Tim was playing in was typical of the rhythm and blues bands that had replaced jazz as the favoured music of the current student crop. They were good, and Tim dutifully played the riffs along with the sax players; however, even I could tell that he was waiting to burst into a solo. When he did, it was with a blues-soaked trumpet that I would remember. Almost the whole audience got the message and began to applaud. We could see the admiration on Johnny's face and the envy on the face of his siblings.

As the gig was coming to an end, we walked over to where the cousins were sitting. Hannah told Johnny her news while I stood silently beside her. Tamsin asked me how my project at the farmhouse was proceeding. God knows how she'd found out about it, as I'm sure Johnny wouldn't have volunteered the information. I explained it was my first experience of managing an important project and my next one would be entirely of my design. I guessed she was somehow trying to undermine me by belittling the work I was doing; I had long since learned that total honesty was the best defence against people trying to scheme against you. I was reluctant to leave Hannah's side, but I wanted to congratulate Tim on his solo. Eventually, he came to join us and I told him how well I thought he'd played.

Hannah had ordered a taxi for eleven, so we left immediately without making long goodbyes. We just wanted to get away. Craig's malignant, silent presence was really difficult to ignore and took the edge off what otherwise would have been a really good evening for Tim and Johnny. I decided I'd ring Tim the next day.

Meanwhile, I had to deal with Hannah, who had descended from elation to a low point, induced by her nauseating cousins. I was desperate to get her home.

"I've suddenly come over very tired," she told me as soon as we'd descended into the basement. "Can we just go to bed?" I went to the kitchen and fetched two glasses of water and, when I came back, she was sitting with her back against the pillows. As I got in beside her, she slid down under the covers and asked if I'd come and hold her. I told her I didn't have anything better to do so I might. An arm came up from beneath the sheets, feeling for mine.

When I got back from work the following evening, she was nearly ready to talk. She asked how my day had been. Ordinary, I told her. Once you get to the scaffold work it's just coat after coat of paint. Seth still had no word about the warehouse job, so I could be next door again soon. I could see she was putting off talking about the night before, so I started.

"Johnny must have been well pissed off last night."

"Oh God, I'm sick of them."

I switched into listening mode, and waited for the story I knew was coming.

"When we were younger, we met all the time, but I came to discover that Craig was odd. I was friendly with Tamsin for a while, then felt the spite that her jealousy of my relationship with Nana produced. I told Nana and she told me I needn't have contact with them if I didn't want to. You can imagine what happened next. Calls to Nana saying I was being standoffish and cruel. Carl was always hovering in the background somewhere. The cousins treated him as if he didn't exist, so when he told Nana what was happening she told Clara that I was too busy with my tutors to play with them any more. Since then, it has mostly been Christmas when we've met; Nana has always felt obliged to carry on with the tradition of the family gathering. As Nana has become older, they have insisted on more contact, and we all know why. Honestly, Peter, I don't want them in my life, but they are family."

I told her Johnny must feel the same.

My family never had money, so we never thought about it much. Dad told me there had been a bit of a falling out among his branch of the family, when it was found that one of his sisters hadn't been paying the life insurance payments his mother had been giving her. In the scheme of things, it was pennies, but when you haven't got many pennies it's a big thing. The row that ensued saw Dad keeping his brother and three sisters at arms' length. He told me that he'd got Mum, her family and us lot and that was all he needed. For this reason, I was keen to bring Sally back into the fold. I didn't know then that she was just the other side of the fence waiting for an invitation.

*

Having converted her MA into a research doctorate, Hannah's deadline had suddenly faded away. I asked about all the work she'd put in and she told me it would form the basis of her thesis.

I'd never given anyone Hannah's number, which was good in some ways, but not in others. On Friday evening, not long after we'd eaten, Hannah's bell rang. I was in the loo, so Hannah went to answer it. When I came out, I could hear lots of laughing female voices coming down the stairs. It was all three of my sisters plus a wickedly smiling Melissa.

"We are all going to The Greyhound for a drink. We thought you'd like to join us."

I nodded to Sally, indicating she join me. We went into the kitchen and I asked if she was alright.

"I did it, Peter, and it was very painful for both of us. You were right: Graham knew it was coming, but it didn't make it any easier. Anyway, can we leave that for now? The jolly duo insisted I come and call on you, and Caroline was desperate to join us. Sorry, little brother, it seems your sisters have come to do what annoying sisters do."

I could hear Hannah laughing, so I knew all was well and told Sally to come and meet Hannah properly. They looked at each other uneasily for a while; then Hannah, who seemed determined to defuse the tension between them, walked across the room and took Sally into a fierce hug.

If there is such a thing as a surplus male, I was one that night. Four women, all with questions to ask and stories to tell, and then there was me. The contrast between Wednesday at the White Hart and that night in The Greyhound couldn't have been missed by Hannah. She was the centre of my sisters' attention, and I loved them for it.

*

Right at the last minute, Seth received the go-ahead for the warehouse conversion. I was to meet the architect on site. The building work was complete, although not to the original spec, which meant bits of my design needed adjusting. I kept my cool; he'd have needed to get the permission off the client to make the changes, so I would have to work with them. The architect told me why they had made the alterations and I had to agree that it made sense. His part of the conversion had been signed off, so it was down to me and my team to finish the project.

I decided I needed a meeting with the client and asked Seth if he'd organise it. After I'd explained why, Seth agreed. It was a couple in their thirties. Where they had raised the money for such an expensive project I could only guess, and my guess was that their parents weren't poor.

The meeting took place at the conversion. The woman was dressed on trend and had plenty of confidence. I knew straight away she'd be the one I'd be dealing with. The guy was trying hard to pay attention, but I felt it was something he had no interest in. We agreed a way around the alterations. I asked for one of them to make site visits every few days. The guy felt he had to explain that this was Sara's project really. Sara gave me their number and I gave her Seth's. Hannah and I had agreed: Seth was the only one I was to give her number to outside of the family. I didn't need to be convinced. The work would start in one week's time, so I would be back at the Crescent for a week.

"Can you take two days off next week before you start the warehouse job?"

"Why?"

"I want you to come to Oxford with me on Tuesday; I need a husband."

"Your supervisor fancies you?"

"Not sure, but I need to know whether, if he does, it in any way influenced the decision to offer me the chance to convert from an MA to a PhD. It's unlikely, because it would have been a committee that approved the offer, but it would have been on his recommendation. I want it to be on merit. It's a big thing getting this chance, but it wouldn't be the first time a woman..."

"Okay, wife, I get the message, but I'm sure you're worrying unnecessarily. I never take time off and we're slack at the moment, so I'll come with you. Seth won't complain."

Seth didn't, and asked if we would come for a meal with him and Joyce on the following Friday. Hannah was keen to go so I said yes.

*

The taxi dropped us at the gates to a small courtyard. It was dark in the narrow street, so I couldn't get a clear picture of the building we were about to enter. Hannah pressed some numbers into a keypad and the lock was released so that we could push the heavy cast iron gates inwards. We crossed to a set of large oak doors and Hannah pressed more numbers. The space beyond was larger than I'd imagined and the lobby walls were all of natural stone. One more door and we were in a lift to the fourth floor. I'd seen plenty of photos of penthouse suites during my studies, but had never set foot in one before. The view over Oxford was impressive. I turned to her and asked the obvious.

"It's owned by the Trust who let it out on my behalf. It was Grandad's, then my father's and now I have use of it. The Trust gave me preference when I started my studies here."

Not long after we got together I'd asked where she stayed when she was in Oxford and she told me it was in a family property. I hadn't given it much more thought.

Now I was standing in it I was beginning to realise just how wealthy Hannah was. Four floors of well designed apartments in the middle of Oxford. Those alone would bring a considerable amount of money into her Trust.

"Sorry, Peter, but I told you Dad left me income from a trust. This is part of it."

"Don't tell me about the other part."

She asked, "Why not?" I explained my thinking. Her finances seemed to be well managed by her Trust and her financial advisors. She was welcome to talk things through with me should a problem arise, but as I knew little about finance I wasn't sure how much use I'd be other than a sounding board.

"Of course, you can tell me about your finances if you feel you need to. I don't want to seem uninterested, but I really want to concentrate on developing my skills as a designer."

She looked at me as if I'd said something incomprehensible.

"You really aren't very interested in money, are you?"

"Hannah, money is something that can make you feel happy or, if you want it too much, as miserable as Tamsin and Craig. I want you to understand that it's you that's making me happy. Anything else that crops up we'll deal with when it does. Do you understand what I'm trying to say?"

"You don't want our relationship fucked up by my money. Is that it?"

"That's one way of putting it, but it's more than that. I don't want money to somehow define our relationship. I want us to remain who we are and, if you haven't worked it out yet, I'm rather fond of you."

"What am I going to do with you, Peter? Come on, put your clothes away and we'll go and eat. There is a good Italian restaurant just around the corner. I booked ahead."

It turned out there was no real reason for me to be in Oxford. When Hannah's supervisor realised she was in Oxford with her partner, he invited us for dinner that evening. His name was Steve and he lived with his academic wife Terri on one of the estates just outside of town. The house was a semi, which was bigger but otherwise much like the one I grew up in. You didn't have to be in their company long to see that they were very together as a couple.

Terri settled us in the lounge while Steve disappeared into a large extension at the back of the house where there was a very modern kitchen. Terri explained that Steve was the house cook and, while she liked cooking, Steve loved it. Hannah explained that it was the other way around at home.

I asked how Terri had met Steve. "At a party. I'd just taken up a post in the History Department teaching the History and Development of Law in Europe. Steve is a sociologist who studies the way the law impacts on society. The study of punishment, restorative justice, imprisonment that sort of thing. We had lots to talk about, but it obviously didn't end there. And you two, how did you meet?"

I nodded to Hannah for her to take the lead, but before she could say anything, Steve came out of the kitchen to tell us everything was ready. He explained they were vegetarians so there would be no meat. We'd started to eat vegetarian food a couple of times a week so it was nothing unusual for us.

It was quite some spread: a mixture of falafel, rissoles and fritters with a variety of sauces and salads. Hannah and Steve discussed cook books for a while and agreed that Rose Elliot had been their starting point. So many new vegetarian books were appearing that it had become difficult to keep pace. Terri asked if I cooked. I told her I didn't. I would take up the challenge, but I was up against someone who had a feel for cooking that I couldn't hope to match. She smiled and asked what I did for a living. Steve and Hannah stopped to hear my response. I told them I worked in interior design. It was Terri who responded. "Really? I've a friend who is looking for someone. Have you a card?"

I told her we rarely worked outside of Bristol but that I would give her a number to ring before we left. The rest of the evening was about their research, followed by the usual small-talk, to which I contributed little. When I was at Hannah's side, I'd come to understand that the best way to learn was to listen. As a result, I gained an insight into Hannah's work and into how a university operated. The next day, Hannah insisted she show me around Oxford before we caught the train home. I was impressed.

CHAPTER 13

It seemed no sooner had we started the warehouse conversion than it was finished. Not having to work around people and their treasured belongings was a big advantage and the work progressed really quickly. We were now receiving enquires at a rate the two of us were struggling to handle. To cope, I took on all the new conversion work. Seth preferred working with clients in period properties, so he focused on that area, plus he handled the initial stages of each enquiry.

Through all this, Hannah and I kept up our nightly habit of exchanging accounts of our daily activities. She travelled to Oxford regularly and sometimes to Edinburgh to meet with Peter Young, a professor in the Law Department and a sociologist who had been one of the founders of British Criminology. I could just about keep up with her studies, but sometimes she told me bluntly I would have to show her my finished projects for her to be able to comment.

The basement had become our haven. I felt some stress at work, but it was just work and nothing a bit of negotiation couldn't put right. Hannah's stress was different, self-imposed and sometimes difficult to handle both for her and for me. Deep in the night, I would wake to find her soaked in sweat, clinging to me tightly and pleading for me not to let go.

It was Saturday, a day we tried to keep work-free, but had lately seen Hannah making excuses to disappear to the office upstairs. I went to the office and found her sitting in front of the screen doing nothing.

"Tell me honestly: why is the PhD so important to you?

She turned on the swivel chair to face me. "It's the last bloody exam, the final one; after that there is nothing and I'm not going to be defeated by it."

"You already are."

"What are you saying, Peter? Are you saying I've already failed?"

"No, Hannah, listen to me! You're clever enough to do what you've set out to do, but you've become obsessed and it has become a monster. You'll hate me for saying this, but it's just a piece of bloody paper. Ninety nine percent of the population doesn't even know what a PhD is. You need to treat it as a job like any other. Do the research, work out if an outcome's possible and, if not, walk away."

"Go away, Peter, just go a-fucking-way!"

I'd said what I needed to say, so I went to the basement, packed an overnight bag and headed for the ancestral home.

Mum didn't say anything when I asked if I could stay over. Apparently, Caroline was never at home so I could have my old room for the night. Sally was surprised to find me there when she arrived home from a Saturday shift. She immediately fell back into big sister mode.

"What's wrong, little Brother? You two can't fall out – you're our last hope for the perfect couple."

"The perfect couple's in the living room, or about as perfect a couple as it gets."

It was then that the hall telephone began to ring. Sally went to answer it. After a minute or two, she called Mum to the phone.

After Mum had put the phone down, she dashed upstairs and emptied her wardrobe onto the bed.

"Sally," she called, "what the hell am I supposed to wear?"

It seemed that Lady Roxford had called to invite my parents, sisters and me to lunch the following day.

I rang Hannah and she eventually picked up. I didn't get the chance to say anything; she just asked me to come home. I wasn't going to rush. I wanted to talk to Mum first. Mum was in a fluster and I needed to stop her worrying. The meal was informal, there was no need for her to worry about what to wear. I could see I was having little effect, so I asked Sally to tell her. Sally did no better than me and suggested that I get Hannah to ring Mum.

*

I left to catch the bus soon after. Buses were going to be a thing of the past for me soon as Seth had organised driving lessons and my test was due in two weeks. Apparently, we were generating enough money between us to justify a second vehicle. We both knew that I needed to drive as I now found myself the lead on several jobs at once and too much time was being wasted getting between them. Hannah was adamant that she was never going to drive. She'd had one lesson and hated it.

When I arrived back, there was a note asking me to head towards the greengrocer she favoured to help carry her bags. I found her in the deli next to the butcher. Nothing was said on the way back to the flat, but I could feel that there was a dam wall about to breach. We emptied the bags onto the kitchen table and she began to sort their contents and place them into the appropriate cupboards. Suddenly she stopped and turned to face me.

"I hate you, Peter Hawker. How can you be so bloody calm all the time?"

"Funny," I said, "I always thought you were the one who was always in control."

"More likely, struggling to stay in control."

I asked if she remembered Gareth, the guy who gave tours of the city. She nodded, and I told Hannah that one evening in the library I mentioned my partner was a PhD student. He told me the most difficult thing about doing original research was the intellectual loneliness of it. By definition, you are attempting something that hasn't been achieved before, so there are very few people you can talk to about what you were doing. I didn't want Hannah to feel lonely and depressed, but I didn't want her to give up. We needed to work on a strategy for when it was getting to her.

"You really think I can do it, don't you?"

"Yes. Now, what's all this with inviting my family for lunch?"

"I think you know."

"Well, maybe; however, Mum is in a panic, so can you please ring her and assure her it's all very casual and she needn't worry about what to wear."

"I'll do it now before I start preparing things for tomorrow. You're going to have to help me."

"Yes, ma'am."

*

Mum had calmed down by the time I spoke to her that evening. I told her we'd be sending a taxi for her and Dad and to be ready by midday. I also mentioned that the food would not be the traditional Sunday lunch, but I had tasted it before and knew she would like it. It had taken a long time for Mum to get used to what she called foreign food. She still referred to spaghetti Bolognaise as worms in mud and just could not handle Chinese food. I was sure she'd like Hannah's version of moussaka, which contained potato instead of aubergine; after all, it was just a Greek relation of shepherd's pie. It seemed that Caroline had a previous engagement, but Jenny was going to be there, no doubt with Melissa in tow.

We were putting the last touches to the salads that would accompany the moussaka, so Hannah and I missed the casual chatter that went with the pre-lunch drinks. When it was ready, I went upstairs to man the top end of the dumbwaiter.

Dad was standing with Carl near the head of the table. Carl's love of cars and Dad's work in engineering gave them plenty to talk about. The women were sitting around Esmé. Mum looked as if she was feeling a little awkward; however, the relentless jolliness of Jenny and Melissa, who treated Esmé as if she was just another nice old lady, eventually took away Mum's tension.

I called them all to the table and Carl did the honours in leading them to their places, after which he came to my side to help deliver the food. When Hannah appeared, it was difficult to imagine she'd just left the kitchen. She took her place next to Mum and Esmé. I was sitting next to Dad, who in turn was sitting next to Carl. Carl was talking enthusiastically about the cars the family had owned in their heyday. I thought Dad seemed genuinely interested, so I turned to Sally who was sitting to my right.

How was she? I could feel she wasn't sure. She told me that some of her friends couldn't understand why she'd split with Graham. She didn't know how, but it seemed that Graham and her breaking up had somehow made them feel threatened or uncomfortable in some way. The end result was that a few of her friends were avoiding her. I didn't quite know what to say. This was an area only the most sensitive blokes wandered into willingly. I told her Hannah and I were trying to keep our weekends free to do new things. If she wanted she should come and join us. She looked doubtful.

It all seemed to have gone well. Esmé had spent a long time talking to Mum and I could see by the way they occasionally gazed in our direction that there was some joke being shared at our expense. The meal seemed to be over quickly and I think even Sally, who wasn't in the best of moods, enjoyed being there.

It was unusual to hear Esmé raise her voice, but when she did it was commanding enough for everyone to listen. She thanked Hannah for cooking the food and everyone for coming; however, one thing was puzzling her. Well, if something was puzzling Esmé, then I for one was curious.

Esmé turned to face Melissa.

Melissa, my dear, since I discovered your surname, I have become a little curious. Please tell us, Miss Altinham, how you are related to the Lady Olivia of that name? Melissa looked at Esmé and smiled. "You've caught me out. I won't deny it: she's my grandma."

"I burst into laughter, while a smiling Jenny told Melissa that she must tell her more of the poor family that she came from over in the East."

I wasn't sure what Mum and Dad made of all this, but I could see that Hannah was not best pleased with Melissa.

After seeing Mum and Dad off, Hannah and I retreated to the basement.

"I can't believe Melissa. All this time, playing at being little Miss Working Class."

"I don't know, Hannah, I think there might be more to the story than her wanting to be seen as something she isn't. Jenny says she only began her post grad work because she managed to secure a grant. She certainly worked hard to get a first on her undergraduate course. I've always felt that Melissa was trying to prove something. I've met guys like her on site. With Melissa, it's humour; with them, it was bravado. Underlying it is something that needs to be confronted. I told you about Cliff. His is one story among many."

"You are so bloody annoying, Peter Hawker. I was beginning to enjoy being pissed off with Melissa and now I am going to have to be her friend and find out what's troubling her."

"I don't think Jenny has succeeded, so I wish you luck with that one."

CHAPTER 14

Johnny rang on the Monday to invite us to dinner the following Friday. They had been to us several times and Johnny had become much more relaxed around Hannah. We both enjoyed their company. Johnny and Tim were quite a double act, always making us laugh, but there was a darker side to Johnny's humour. The way he imitated Craig was accurate and disturbing. I asked him about it and he said he found his brother scary at times, but not in any really nasty way. He'd tried, but couldn't get through to him. Only Tamsin could do that.

When we arrived on the Friday, Tim spent ages apologising to Hannah about the food. Tim said it was a Bolognese, but would be nothing like the one they cooked in Bologna. Hannah laughed and insisted she was not a purist, telling Tim cookery was an art and the best cooks were the ones most willing to experiment. It didn't stop Tim from looking a little nervous when he brought the food to the table.

I asked why they hadn't called about the gigs Tim had been playing at. Johnny answered, saying that he'd stopped going to Tim's gigs regularly because Craig and Tamsin had started to show up every time Tim was playing. He'd guessed that Hannah wouldn't be keen on going if they were there. I suggested they let us know anyway. Hannah was often busy with her studies and I didn't have any big projects at the planning stage, so I was free in the evenings. I wasn't going to be intimidated by the presence of Tamsin and Craig.

Hannah was in Oxford the following week and I missed her. When she wasn't at home her absence made me think about how well I really knew her. In many people's eyes, we were still the most improbable of couples. People didn't say so outright, but when Hannah introduced me to a new acquaintance you could see they were puzzled. Dad, who was totally useless when I was making my transition from boy to man, had recently taken to giving me advice. Well, perhaps some second-hand advice he'd got from his father. They had both had long marriages, so I paid attention. His opening statement was a bit of a surprise.

"You'll never really know Hannah. You do realise that, don't you?"

To be honest, I didn't. I thought that Mum and Dad had been together so long they knew each other inside out and that if Hannah and I stayed together for long enough we would be the same. Not true, according to Dad; if you thought like that you would begin to take one another for granted and that never ended well.

"There will always be some part of her you will never know and it's probably better you don't. The same applies to her with regard to you. She will surprise you in some way when you least expect it. Don't become complacent."

I couldn't see the things he was telling me about in his relationship with Mum, which I guess is the first lesson I needed to learn. Never assume you know what's going on in other people's lives and never become complacent about what's going on in your own.

Hannah got all philosophical on me once and wondered if it was me she'd fallen in love with or a version of me she'd constructed in her head. I told her that what she saw was all there was and she laughed, shaking her head in disagreement. It made me think that maybe we are all capable of constructing a version of the people we love, which when it comes down to it doesn't match their reality. Perhaps that was what Dad meant when he said I would never really know Hannah.

*

Suddenly shifting from a seat at the front of a bus to a seat behind the wheel of a van came as a bit of a shock. I hadn't studied the Highway Code as much as I should have and my instructor was convinced I wasn't ready. Seth had given me a few lessons and was convinced I was. On the day of the test I felt surprisingly relaxed. Just as well really, for the test route I was used to driving had suddenly become an obstacle course. There were road works and at the junction to the main road the traffic lights had failed. The examiner watched me closely as I negotiated each obstacle. When we arrived back at the testing station, he asked me a few cursory questions about the Highway Code then congratulated me on passing my test. Seth told me that showing you were capable of dealing with the unexpected almost guaranteed a pass.

The van Seth found for me was a tidy Bedford HA. They'd been around for a while and were cheap and sort of reliable. It made my life so much easier, but having use of a van comes with all sorts of requests for favours. Tim, who now had his own jazz quintet, was always in need of help to move some of his band's kit. I obliged when I could, but tried not to make myself too available. Hannah was not keen on the van as she complained she couldn't stretch her legs in the tiny front cabin. She could afford taxis, so I didn't complain when she insisted we use one.

Johnny and Hannah were becoming closer and I was pleased that she had at least one cousin she could relate to. However, Tamsin and Craig were never far from our minds. The one thing that nagged at mine was something Esmé had said – "If anything happens to Hannah, then they will inherit, as I have no other relatives." I tried hard not to think anyone capable of harming Hannah, but, shit, Craig was a complete unknown. I was going to have to work on this. Maybe I was being a bit paranoid, but I needed to find out more about Craig and just how much of a threat he posed, if any. If I didn't, it would play on my mind and Hannah would soon feel that something was bothering me. It was going to be difficult as Craig hardly spoke when I was in his company. Maybe I could try and find out more from Johnny.

We'd planned a visit to my parents on the Saturday. I wanted to check up on Sally as I hadn't seen her for a while. We arrived at the same time Sally returned from her morning shift. Hannah took Sally aside while I spoke to Mum and Dad. Mum was a bit worried about Caroline as she was never home on weekends, but I knew she was doing alright. She was still hanging out with Ian, the folk musician. We had met him and Caroline at The Greyhound on a night out with Jenny and Melissa. He seemed quite shy, but came alive when he started to play his guitar. I didn't think Mum was convinced, but my lack of worry seemed to ease her mind a little.

Hannah came back into the living room alone and, when I gave her a quizzical look, she explained that Sally had gone to pack an overnight bag. She was coming with us to see Tim play tonight and it would be easier if she stayed over. I said my goodbyes and went to clear a space in the back of the van for Sally.

*

We arrived early at the Arts Centre to make sure we had a place to sit. Natalie and Leon were sitting half way down the room and called for us to join them. We pushed two tables together and, after finding out what people were drinking, I recruited Sally to help me carry the drinks back from the bar.

"Isn't this a bit awkward for you all?" Sally asked.

I told her no. I'd never really got it together with Natalie and, anyway, why should she worry about choosing the handsome Leon over me? Sally laughed and told me that I was a complete idiot. As we were walking back, I saw Gareth, the self-taught historian from the library, standing at the bar. I dropped off the drinks at the table and went to speak to him. When I discovered he was there alone, I asked him to join us. He asked if I was sure. Absolutely, I replied. I knew he could be a bit over-enthusiastic about his subject, but did seem to register when his audience couldn't take any more.

Johnny arrived with Tim; there was no sign of Craig or Tamsin. He joined us while Tim went to help with the sound check. Sally knew about modern jazz from all the LPs I played at home. I wasn't quite sure what she'd make of Tim's quintet, though.

When the band was ready, Tim announced there would be three short sets with breaks for the bar in between. He raised a laugh when he asked if there were any complaints and if people preferred they play one unbroken set.

~ 136 ~

I don't read music and I don't know the reason I fell in love with jazz. However, I had the knowledge of a true fan. The alto sax player was obviously a disciple of Art Pepper as much as Tim was of Chet Baker. This was the West Coast version of what was happening on the East Coast of America back in the fifties, and to my mind it was so much cooler. I looked around the table and everyone was listening intently. Tim once told me that applause is good, but knowing people really get what you're doing is better. Most of us sitting around that table did.

The first break gave Hannah and me a chance to catch up with Natalie and Leon. I kept looking back to Sally, but Gareth seemed to have her attention. Leon was doing site work; less dust, he explained, and he had quickly advanced to foreman. It wasn't what he'd planned, but he was doing alright.

I could see that Natalie was really curious about Hannah and me. That night, she wouldn't learn a lot. Oddly, it seemed that while I bore no grudge, Hannah felt that Natalie had been a bit unfair not ending our relationship face to face. It was going to take a while.

While Sally was at the bar with me, Hannah took the opportunity to move next to Gareth. I knew Gareth had a strong interest in Royal York Crescent and I'd told Hannah about it. When we arrived back at the table, I could see he was gently questioning her to find out just how much she knew about the place where she lived. I think they must have surprised one another with their enthusiasm.

After the final set, Hannah and I said our goodbyes to the others and, with Gareth and Sally, set out on the walk back to Clifton. Gareth told us he was doing a tour of Clifton Wood the following afternoon and asked if any of us would like to come. Hannah seemed quite keen and, to my surprise, so did Sally. It was agreed we'd go and I would run Sally home in the van after Gareth's tour was finished.

*

Clifton is divided roughly into three areas: Clifton Down, Clifton Village and Clifton Wood. Coming from an estate lacking a posh name, I found it amusing that the people of Clifton, who to a man and woman lived in a suburb consisting of Georgian or Victorian buildings, had somehow convinced themselves they lived either in a village or a wood. Gareth's tour was enlightening. At the time, Clifton was largely run down, full of student lets and pubs full of academics, writers and wannabe hippy intellectuals. There were a few of the original families hanging on, but only just.

We met at The Lion in Clifton Wood, and all found drinks and seats while Gareth gave us the lowdown on what he knew of the architects and builders. He also had some interesting anecdotes he'd gained from workers. Unlike the grand Georgian terraces in the Village, it seemed the terraces of Clifton Wood had been built largely by Victorian spec builders, some of whom had cut a lot of corners. One member of a renovating team had told Gareth that the second floor of the house he was working in was sitting on joists of two inches by seven inches, a half the width they should have been. On top of this, they had been drilled full of holes for gas lighting, then electricity cables and indoor plumbing. He had no idea why the whole floor had not collapsed. The guy had told the developer about it and was told that it wasn't his worry.

Gareth had a wealth of these stories and, as we walked along Clifton Wood Terrace, it was easy to believe he'd been inside every one of the houses and knew them well. As we neared the end of the terrace, Gareth stopped us and told us the tale of a builder who was called to the house we'd just passed. Inside, he told us, lived an old lady who had been there all her life. She had outlived her sons, who were casualties of war, and had eventually ended up living on the ground floor. However, she could not afford essential repairs nor ignore forever the drips coming through the ceiling, so she eventually called the Council for help. Consistent complaints from neighbours eventually brought a Council officer and a building inspector. What they found alarmed them.

The central valley roof rested on a single beam that stretched from the front to the back of the building. When the Council officers entered the long abandoned back bedroom, they saw that the beam had rotted away from where it was sitting on the back wall and had dropped three inches onto the top of an old Victorian mahogany wardrobe. It was the only thing holding the roof up. It seems Victorian builders may have cut corners, but Victorian cabinet makers built well.

Gareth had a tour of the area surrounding Royal York Crescent planned for Sunday week. We all agreed to go. Hannah invited Sally to come on the Saturday and she would cook a meal. As an afterthought, she turned and asked Gareth if he would like to join us for supper. Gareth looked surprised but readily agreed.

*

I never got the chance to talk to Johnny about Craig at the gig and it was going to be a while before the next one. Without any tangible reason, Craig was beginning to worry me. I just had this creeping feeling that life was too good at the moment. Something bad was bound to happen.

I needed to finish a sketch and detail for another conversion. This time it was an old stable block on one of the farms that had slowly been surrounded by the city. The client had agreed with the architect to a plan along modernist lines, so Seth had dropped it in my in tray. It was just initial designs, but they were still going to take me two days. Hannah had moved out of her nana's office and into the empty room next door. We shared it, as we somehow managed to work beside each other without too much friction. Hannah was in Oxford that day so I had the office to myself.

The room overlooked the road in front of the Crescent. I was staring out of the window absent-mindedly when I spotted her. It was Tamsin standing across the road looking up at the house. She seemed to be hesitant, then finally began to cross the road. I made a quick phone call to the hall phone next door and asked the builder if Melissa was in her room. He called her to the phone and I asked her to come to the basement as soon as she could. I told her I would owe her. She laughed. I was in time to answer the door.

"Tamsin, this is a surprise."

"Well, Peter, if I wanted to speak to you it wouldn't be any good waiting for an invitation, now would it? Let's at least start by being honest."

"Okay, come down and I'll put the kettle on."

I was unsure what Tamsin wanted to talk to me about until she made it plain she wanted to talk about the future, her future in particular. I'd asked Melissa to come down because I wasn't sure what to expect and I really did not want to be left alone with Tamsin. When Melissa came bouncing down the stairs, I began to introduce her. "No need," Tamsin told us. "I know who Melissa is." Melissa ignored the tinge of malice in Tamsin's tone and said she'd be down later with Jenny. I thanked her and she headed off up the stairs.

"Got a thing about Ladies' granddaughters have you?"

"Come on, Tamsin, tell me why you're here or piss off. I haven't got time for the games the upper middle-class are so fucking fond of."

"Don't be so touchy. I'm here to tell you I'm giving up babysitting Craig. I've spent a lifetime doing a job that my mother should have been doing and I am not doing it any more. I've got a place at York University to study Chemistry, and nothing is going to stop me from going."

"Congratulations, so why are you telling me?"

"Why do you think?"

"Is Craig a problem?"

"How the fuck should I know?"

"You must know, otherwise you wouldn't be here."

"He's obsessive, but I know he wouldn't harm anyone, especially Hannah."

"So why are you here?"

"I don't know. I'm leaving town, just watch out."

"For what?"

"Listen to me, Peter, Mum spent all her time grooming Johnny and found out too late that he was gay. I know that Craig resents her for that. Dad is just a wet sponge and does exactly as he's told. Craig does nothing. He just hangs around watching TV. He could have gone to university. He has plenty of A levels, but he seemed to give up as soon as he'd finished sixth form. He's become more and more introverted. He used to talk to me; now when I ask him something he just grunts in response. Mum has filled our heads with nonsense since we were young. Lord Roxford actually tried to help us when Grandad fucked up, but according to her he just did it because he felt guilty about not making Grandad disinvest in Wall Street before it crashed. Just how was he supposed to do that, I asked her? She won't listen. Resents living off the Trust money, but does nothing about it. Well, I'm getting out; I don't want to be beholden to anyone. I've seen where it's led Mum. I've got a grant and I'll live off that and work in a bar to pay my rent."

"What are you trying to tell me, Tamsin?"

"I don't know why Hannah has moved you in, but believe me it won't last. It may be fashionable to have a working-class lover at the moment, but when it comes to making babies you can bet your life it'll be with someone from her own class."

"Thank you, Tamsin," I said with a smile on my face.

I wished her good luck with her studies, and led her to the door. I was definitely not going to show any sign that she'd wound me up, which had obviously been the purpose of her visit. As for Craig, she had left me none the wiser. During the few times I'd been in his company, it seemed obvious that he was a troubled man. As for Tamsin's comments about Hannah, they didn't bother me because I'd received reassurance from someone much closer to her.

*

I always kept the office door open when I was working, and one day Esmé appeared at it and asked if we could talk for a while. I could always claim to be behind with my work as there was so much of it, but I guessed Esmé had a reason for wanting to talk and I cheerily agreed. I was probably doing a lot more hours than Seth was paying me for so I didn't feel guilty about taking a break. Of course, Esmé knew that I wouldn't turn her down and, as soon as she was seated, Carl arrived with two mugs of tea and a tray of biscuits, then left us to it.

Esmé didn't waste time. She was there to find out how I was feeling about Hannah and me. I wasn't quite sure why she was asking and told her so. She had no doubts about Hannah's feelings for me, but it had been a while now and what she wanted to know was if I was having doubts about Hannah's feelings for me and how I felt about Hannah. Before I told her, I wanted to know why she was asking. This was her answer.

"When I was a young woman, Peter, it would have been impossible for me or any other girl of my class, or as we used to like to call it 'social standing', to go out with someone like you. We never mixed with people outside our class and it was expected that we would marry within our social circle, often to someone we were directed to by our mothers. I had my own struggle, for my husband wasn't a lord when I met him. He was middle-class but not quite upper middle-class enough for my mother, who was totally against our getting married. I had to remind her that we were not from some mythical, ancient noble line. Mother's family had made their money in India as part of the East India Company. Before that they had been privateers, pirates raiding Spanish ships with the permission, and to the benefit, of the Crown.

"Women had no economic independence in those days, so if you didn't go with your father's wishes – which were often your mother's by proxy – you were literally cast adrift. Fortunately for me, my father was fond of Reginald and believed he would do well. He ignored my mother and gave me permission to marry. At that time, it would have been difficult if not impossible to marry without my father's consent. Mother only fully forgave me when Reginald was made a baron: a non hereditary peer raised for his service to industry. While the title died with him, I am entitled to retain mine until I die."

She must have thought I was slightly puzzled at her telling me all this, because she carried on by saying, "You may be wondering what the point of all this is. It's quite simple: Hannah is part of a generation free of all the social restraints women suffered in the past. She is economically independent, has control over her own fertility and can do more or less as she pleases. She has achieved a lot and will achieve more. However, the one thing I am really pleased about is that she is happy. You may have doubts that such happiness can last and I cannot predict the future, but for now, Peter, you can reassure me by telling me how you really feel about Hannah."

I could see things in Esmé that I saw in her granddaughter. Her concern for other people's happiness was one of them. She'd asked if I had doubts about Hannah's feelings for me. To be honest, I hadn't given it much thought. I'm not the sort to dwell on such things unless I feel something's amiss. Hannah was happy and so was I. We had the occasional minor difference, but what couple didn't. I got what Esmé was saying about our backgrounds, but so far it had not been an issue and I couldn't see why it should become one. I told her all this and thanked her for coming to see me, then added that my feelings for Hannah were the same as on the day I woke up and realised I'd fallen.

When Hannah got back from Oxford that evening, I told her about Tamsin's visit. I explained about Tamsin going to York and her vague warnings, but I left out the bit about her telling me that Hannah would ditch me to have her children with some posh geezer. We were eating with Seth and Joyce that night and I didn't want to darken the mood any further. Hannah asked what I thought Tamsin was getting at. I told her that I honestly didn't know and that I thought Tamsin was just being malicious.

We had eaten with Seth and Joyce a few times. Hannah had quickly become friends with Joyce, but found it difficult to warm to Seth. Seth's main interest was the business, and I found it hard to move him away from talking about it. It led to segregated evenings, with Seth talking to me about ongoing projects and Hannah and Joyce talking about art and ethnic fabric design. A group conversation only started in the last minutes of the evening and it normally included hints from Seth that Hannah should invest in the business. Hannah had repeatedly told him that at this point in time she had an income but no access to capital.

That evening followed a similar pattern, but when Seth raised the investment issue, Hannah pointedly ignored him and turned to Joyce, asking if Seth ever listened to anything other people said. Joyce laughed and told her probably not.

*

After Tamsin's visit, I realised I needed to get Johnny's take on Craig, so I arranged we go for an early evening beer at the White Hart. Johnny listened while I tried to make sense of Tamsin's visit. He agreed that Craig had become a bit more reclusive in the last couple of years but didn't really think he was harmful. As far as Johnny knew, he was obsessed with ornithology, and had been since his dad had bought him a camera and taken him out bird-watching. In some ways, Johnny told me, Craig was much like Teddy. He suggested that Tamsin was just trying to wind me up. She had always been envious of Hannah and getting at me was a way of getting at her. That made sense, so I put my worries about Craig on the back burner and carried on with life.

*

Hannah never seemed worried or tense when she was cooking for others, but she did like to be on her own in the kitchen. I used the time to read. Hannah had directed me to books on sociology and philosophy that she thought were essential, and I had finally got around to reading them. Having someone who could explain the bits I found confusing was useful, though I had to pick my times. I could tell by the expression on Hannah's face when her mind was too occupied to be bothered by questions from me. Sally was due shortly and I suspected Gareth would probably arrive early. I'd laid the table and sorted the drinks. So everything was ready.

I was right about Gareth. He did arrive early and he seemed a bit agitated. I asked him what was wrong but he claimed there was nothing. We sat for a while in front of the fire. He was quiet, almost reflective, which was unusual. Gareth normally had plenty to talk about and once he got started didn't stop. Tonight he seemed to be pacing himself. He told me that he must have looked at the houses in Royal York Crescent a thousand times, but this was the first time he'd been invited into one.

At the sound of the bell, I stood up to let Sally in. I took her overnight bag and went to kiss her on both cheeks before I stopped myself and questioned how that had become a habit. A bit obvious, really. Sally had guessed what I was about to do and kissed me cheekily on my nose, telling me that I should watch out, for I was turning into the sort of prat I had always taken the piss out of.

Gareth's smile broadened as we came down the stairs. He stood and made to kiss Sally on both cheeks, she returned the gesture then turned to me and winked. I was thinking I was missing something, when a call from the kitchen interrupted my thoughts. Hannah told me to get them seated and then return to help carry the food. I think one glass of wine was all it took for Gareth to lose the agitation I'd felt in him when he arrived. Sally led the conversation by asking about Gareth's past and his passion for architecture. I was surprised to learn that he'd been a pupil at the nearby grammar school. A posh place that took day students as well as boarders. He explained that, although he did well academically, his experience there was not positive. Sally asked why and he told her that basically it was down to the fact that he didn't play rugby or cricket and refused to join the cadets. Hannah asked what the cadets were, and Gareth explained that it was an organisation under the wing of the Ministry of Defence, which acted as a recruitment ground for the military. "Boys playing at being soldiers," he told us. Gareth's family had lost many relatives in the last war so militarism was something he hated. I wanted to know what he did now. He told us he was a librarian in a

Catholic boys' school in the south of the city, trying to guide the pupils to books that would help them grow into civilised human beings. I was warming to Gareth by the minute and got the feeling I wasn't the only one.

Meal over, we'd settled into an after-dinner glass of red. The sitting room in the basement was cosy and warm and the log fire produced the sort of atmosphere that might send you to sleep if you weren't paying attention. Sally was gently questioning Gareth. Hannah stayed quiet and indicated I should do the same. That evening, I learnt a lot about Gareth, but I probably learnt more about my oldest sister. When Gareth announced he was leaving, Sally volunteered to show him out while I helped Hannah to clear the table and sort out the dishes. It was a while before Sally returned, and I mentioned she'd been gone for a while. She turned to me and smiled, saying, "Yes, I have, little Brother, haven't I?" I took the hint. Hannah was giving me the look I'd come to recognise as 'honestly, please don't be so dull'.

*

Gareth's tour started at eleven the following morning. We met at the end of Cornwallis Crescent, which consists of twenty-four flat-fronted Georgian houses undergoing a patchy process of renovation. I'd worked in a flat at the Polygon Lane end of the Crescent when I started with Seth. The guy who owned it worked for the BBC and had a lot of confidence. He had the sort of voice that indicated he'd been to some posh school somewhere. I decided then that it was all well and good being confident, but it was only really useful if you had something to be confident about. This guy was as shallow as a puddle after a brief summer shower. Trying to tell Seth something he obviously knew more about than the guy telling him was never going to go down well, and I was truly glad when the job was over with.

There appeared little that Gareth didn't know about Cornwallis Crescent: its architecture or its more famous residents. From there, we walked along York Gardens towards the far end of Royal York Crescent. For someone who had never been invited into one of the houses, Gareth seemed to know a lot about their internal configuration and the people who had lived in them. We ended up in the Coronation Tap, a cider pub that Hannah told me she had never been in before. Gareth, on the other hand, seemed well acquainted with the landlord. He told me later that the pub was a great place for gathering stories about that part of Clifton.

I can't remember how it came up. I think I was asking about early photos of the area. He told me that there was a little archive of photographs in the museum, but there must be thousands more. People were always taking pictures of the Crescents. There was one guy in particular who he often saw around ours. "He carries the sort of kit you'd expect a photographer of the natural world would carry. Expensive Nikon cameras and long lenses. You know: kit for distance rather than wide angle?" I didn't, and asked him what the guy looked like. Average height with fairish hair, was the best he could manage. I asked myself if it could be Craig and what he might be up to. I decided that it was important I find out. It might not be him, so Hannah didn't need to know just yet.

*

I was on my own for the first part of the following week as Hannah had travelled up to Edinburgh for a conference on the Effectiveness of Education in Prisons. Her thesis was focused on rehabilitation and she thought it would be useful for her to be there. She left in the afternoon, so I said my goodbyes in the morning. When I got back from work, I found a note on the basement door. It was from Melissa. She asked if she and Jenny could come down that evening for a chat. I didn't mind; work was the only other option.

*

It was just Melissa who rang the bell that evening. She told me that Jenny would be down later. I invited her in, took the bottle of red wine she proffered and went to the kitchen for a corkscrew and two glasses. I noted the label on the bottle: Marqués de Riscal, a Rioja, and not a cheap one. We settled on opposite sofas and I asked what the visit was about. Melissa was quiet for a while.

"I've told Jenny, and didn't want to bore her with it again; now I want to tell you. I know Hannah thinks me a fraud, but I'm not sure you do. I thought I'd stand a better chance with you. So, will you listen?"

I knew there was a lot more to Melissa than the bits she chose to show the world and I told her so. She told me she'd guessed.

"I can understand why Hannah went for you. You can see through the surface to the person."

"Can I?"

"You probably don't know you're doing it, but you can."

"So, what is it you want to tell me?"

"I come from a working family over in the East."

"So how does this fit in with Grandma, Lady Olivia?"

"Easy really: she may be my grandma, but she wouldn't recognise me if she passed me on the street."

I had a definite soft spot for Melissa and I think she had one for me. One of those occasions where a man and woman felt comfortable being friends. This is the story she told me.

Melissa's mother was the youngest of three daughters and, according to Lady Olivia, she should have been a boy. When a third girl arrived, Olivia swore she'd have no more children. Melissa's mother was resented right from the start. They named her Roberta, a boy's name with an 'a' stuck on the end of it. Melissa's mother hated it. Nothing Roberta did was right, so in the end she gave up trying to please Olivia and adopted a strategy of being awkward, embarrassing her mother as much as she could. The final straw was when Roberta fell pregnant and refused to name the father. Olivia was furious about having an unmarried mother for a daughter. Roberta's dad was sympathetic but could not resist the onslaught of pressure from Olivia that led them to disown and disinherit Roberta. I asked Melissa how Roberta managed after she'd been kicked out.

"That's the beautiful bit," Melissa told me. "When Dad found out Mum was pregnant and had been kicked out, he contacted her straight away. He wanted them to get married before my brother was born, but Mum wouldn't hear of it. My dad, Geoff, is a handsome man from a family of market traders. When Dad's father heard about it and realised he was about to become a grandfather, he consulted the family and Mum was allowed to stay in a flat over one of their shops with her baby son. Dad never gave up on Mum and quietly courted her until she gave up and let him move in. Shortly after that, I was born.

They still live in the same flat. I couldn't imagine having more loving parents. Mum gave us our name and refused to marry, until Geoff finally wore her down. Jenny and I will be going to their wedding in the summer.

"I'm sorry, Peter. You know I like to play games, but you're part of my family now and I'm not going to tease you any more. I want you and Hannah to come with me and Jenny to my parents' wedding."

The bell rang and we both stood up to answer it, but before we did Melissa caught me in a tight hug.

"Well, will you come?"

I hugged her back and it was all that was needed; she rushed up the stairs to let my sister in.

*

Hannah got the story when she arrived home from Edinburgh. She didn't seem totally surprised as Esmé had asked some old friends about the Altinham family and picked up on a rumour that Olivia had disowned one of her daughters. I told Hannah about our invite to Melissa's parents' wedding. She didn't seem very enthusiastic, but said she'd go. I thought she was just distracted, and didn't realise until later that this was an indication that something was wrong.

CHAPTER 15

Life had been going on more or less as normal, with Hannah and me exchanging our daily news over evening meals. Hannah's work seemed to be progressing well, as was mine. She had been annoyed with Seth for not offering me a partnership in the firm, but had stopped mentioning it. I was confident that Seth would come up with an offer soon. Seth had an eighteen-month waiting list and we were finding it hard to recruit skilled, reliable decorators. I was now spending more than half my time on project design, which meant sometimes working from Seth's new office and occasionally from the office at home.

I had been keeping an eye out for the mysterious photographer that Gareth had mentioned, but hadn't seen anyone with the sort of expensive cameras he'd described. It was one of those days when I was working from home that I spotted Craig. He was heading towards the front door of a four-storey office block on the other side of the road at the very end of the terrace. It looked like he was carrying a bag of camera equipment. I watched to see what might happen next.

It was fifteen minutes or so before I saw someone moving across the roof and the glint of sunlight on what might have been a camera lens. It was the perfect spot for photographing anyone entering or leaving the house. The question was why would anyone, even Craig, want to do that? There was only one way to find out. I went down the stairs into the basement, through the kitchen door, and across the garden into the back lane. The lane exited from the back of the terrace onto the road opposite the side of the office block. By keeping close to the building, I could get to the front door without being seen from above.

The building's lobby had metal mail boxes down one side and a notice board on the other with posts about fire drills. Each office occupant was listed on a separate board. There was no sign of a building supervisor, so I made my way up the stairs toward the top floor. If I hadn't known the offices were occupied, I'd have thought the place empty. Apart from the distant sound of typewriter keys, the place was remarkably quiet. There was a fire door on the top floor landing that had been left slightly ajar. I went through and found a short set of stairs leading to a small landing within a box-like structure on the roof. The door out was wedged open.

From there, I could see Craig kneeling in front of a small tripod topped by a camera which appeared to be aimed over the low wall at our front door. I walked up slowly behind him, hoping he wouldn't hear my footsteps. When I was close enough I asked, "Any interesting birds down there, Craig?"

Startled, he turned with an embarrassed expression which quickly turned into an angry one.

"I can take photos from wherever I want to but, if you want to know, there have been rumours of a pair of peregrine falcons nesting nearby preying on the pigeon population in Royal York Gardens."

"Bullshit; if I went to your camera now, I know where it would be focused."

He deliberately swung it to one side.

"Believe what you like, but what I do is none of your business, so why don't you just fuck off."

"Because it is my business, Craig. I want to know what you're up to and I want to know now!"

"You don't deserve Hannah. You're just an uncouth, working-class lout. I don't know why she chose you, but maybe she's already changed her mind."

Craig started packing his camera and kit away as quickly as he could.

"What the fuck do you mean by that?"

"You pitiful bastard; ask Hannah about the man that's been visiting her on Thursday afternoons for the past three weeks when you weren't there."

"You're a liar, Craig."

"The camera never lies, fool."

With this, he took a photo from his pocket and flicked it toward me. It fluttered to the floor and, as I bent to pick it up, he pushed me to the ground and ran towards the stairs. I got to the door seconds before he managed to shut it and lock me out. It would have been pointless chasing after him, so I stopped to take a look at the photo. It was of Hannah welcoming a man into the house with some of her air kisses.

I wasn't angry, just deeply upset. I knew the photo was a recent one because next door had just changed the colour of their railings. We'd sat together every evening exchanging news, even trivial daily stuff, but the guy in the photo didn't feature in any of our exchanges. I knew Craig was the first to want me gone and was being malicious, but why would he lie about the guy visiting on Thursdays. He knew I'd ask Hannah. For the first time in my adult life, I felt totally overwhelmed by emotion. I needed answers and I needed them quickly, so I went back to the house and straight to Esmé. I showed her the photo and asked if she knew who the man was. I could see she was uncomfortable. She told me she couldn't tell me, that I would have to ask Hannah. I couldn't face it and told Esmé that Hannah would know where to find me when and if she wanted to explain. Esmé must have seen the tears in my eyes as I left to pack a bag and go.

Two days went by and nothing. Every time the telephone rang, my nerves began to rattle. When it got to Friday, I'd given up. That's it, I thought; it's over and I'd better get used to it, but I wasn't getting over it and I wouldn't. Sally tried to talk to me, but I wasn't listening. When the phone rang, I always let someone else answer. It was Mum who called me to the phone that evening, telling me it was Esmé.

"I shouldn't be calling you, Peter, but I can't stand the thought of you both being so miserable. What's been happening is not what you think and you really must talk to Hannah. I've never known Hannah looking so broken. Come early tomorrow and I will tell you where she is. Come prepared for a journey and bring some overnight clothes. She needs you, Peter; she really does."

I didn't ask why, just said I'd be there in the morning. Whatever happened, at least I would know where I stood. I really loved Hannah, but everyone knows that love is a pointless exercise if the object of your love doesn't love you back.

I needed someone to talk to, so I opened up to Sally. She was shocked at the detail and wouldn't believe that Hannah was capable of being so cruel. Sally said to be patient and when I did meet Hannah I was to let her talk.

"She already knows how you feel, Peter. I've seen how you are with each other and I just can't understand how this has happened. If she's as broken as Esmé says she is, give her the space to say what she needs to."

That made me think. I'd been so miserable and self-absorbed, I hadn't paid much attention to Sally lately. I asked her how she was.

"I'm doing well. Gareth asked me to thank you for introducing us."

"You and Gareth?"

"Don't look so surprised. He's a really interesting man and we are good friends."

"Is that what they're calling it nowadays?"

"Peter!"

"I am happy for you, Sis; Gareth is a really nice guy."

"Hang on, Peter, we are just friends at the moment. Let's see what happens?"

*

On Saturday morning I was up early and was ringing the bell at Royal York Crescent at nine o'clock. Carl answered and handed me an address and a set of instructions of how to get there.

"You must help Hannah, Peter. I know you're upset, but just listen to her; it will mean so much to Esmé."

I looked at the address. It was for a cottage in North Devon. Carl gave me a breakdown of how to get there. It was going to be a four-hour drive in the old Bedford HA. A long drive that would seem even longer with thoughts of what was waiting for me there. I said goodbye and headed for the A38 and my journey south.

North Devon was new to me, and I felt like I was driving into the middle of nowhere. If there was a straight road in that county, I never found it. It was almost impossible for me to overtake anyone or anyone to overtake me. So I just patiently followed the car in front while constantly checking my watch for the time.

I'd been driving along a single-track road for a while before I spotted the farmyard Esmé had mentioned in her notes. Just around the corner was the field gate I was looking for. Carl had told me that the way to the cottage was nothing more than a track across a field, and so it was. I opened the gate, drove through it, then got out to close it behind me. The track was more suited to a Land Rover than an old van. I drove slowly over the bumpy track, trying not to panic the sheep, until I reached a point where the field turned into a steep slope that dropped all the way down to the sea. The view before me was dramatic. I was parked high above a long beach and in the distance I could make out the island of Lundy.

The track down to the cottage was just a grassy slope. I wasn't sure the van would make it back up, so I left it parked on a piece of level ground. With my nerves jangling, I walked down towards the building that was tucked away in a little dip in the land. It was a bungalow of brick and slate and not the small cottage I was expecting. The sign on the gate read West Glyn, so I knew I was in the right place.

I called Hannah's name, but there was no reply. I tried a door and it opened. No way was I going in uninvited, so I decided I'd wait for Hannah's return. An hour later, I saw her walking up the hill from the beach carrying a surfboard. It was a long, steep climb over rough ground littered with sheep droppings. I watched her weave her way through the gorse and thought about going to help, but then thought better of it. It would be hard for her to walk away from me on that steep hill. I decided to wait.

When she finally arrived, she didn't seem surprised and just dropped the surfboard on the grass and stood looking at me. I could see the tears streaming down her face.

"I knew you would come. You had to, Peter, you really had to."

I couldn't keep the tears from my eyes and felt like I was going to start sobbing.

"Tell me, Hannah – just tell me."

She indicated I should follow her into the bungalow and, asking me to give her a few minutes, disappeared into one of the other rooms. When she came back she'd changed from her swimsuit into jeans and a T-shirt. The skin around her eyes was red and blotchy and I could see she was struggling to find her voice. I thought of Sally's advice: "Let her talk, Peter, and, for God's sake, listen and don't interrupt."

"I'm listening, Hannah; please just tell me."

"It wasn't supposed to happen like this. I've totally screwed things up and ended up hurting you when it was the exact opposite I wanted."

Then, as if she'd guessed I'd been thinking of my big sister, she told me that I always had Sally to go to when something was weighing on my mind.

"Peter, the guy in the picture Craig gave you is my therapist. I was his patient before, just for a brief time when I was an undergraduate. It was by sheer chance that I met him on the train on my way back from Edinburgh.

I told him I had a lot on my mind and he suggested I consult him professionally if I thought it would help. I said I would but I didn't want to go to his office, so he agreed to visit me."

I didn't understand why she couldn't tell me what was troubling her. I just couldn't get my head around the fact that she felt she had to keep her meetings a secret. I asked her why.

"It was too big, Peter. I'd done something crazy. I knew I would have to tell you, but I needed to get everything straight in my mind. I was afraid of how you'd react. It just seemed opportune my meeting James on the train. Anyway, the photo Craig gave you was taken at the beginning of the last session I had with him. I was ready to tell you, but I'd left it too late."

I asked her what was too big, what was the crazy thing she'd done?

"Peter, I wasn't happy with the way we were."

I was expecting something like this, but before I could say anything she indicated I should wait and listen.

"Please don't look at me like that, Peter, just let me explain. I wanted more, but I'd seen other women betrayed by men and I didn't trust any of them until I met you. Even then I was nervous, just waiting for you to walk away, and I couldn't go on like that. I knew you were different but, God, I was a total mess inside. Without reason and in an act of wild emotional wilfulness, I stopped taking the Pill. It was stupid of me and now I think I'm pregnant. Peter, I wanted us to get married and share everything no matter what, but now I've put you into a position where you might feel you have to say yes. I wouldn't blame you if you walked away. I've fucked up and I hate myself for it, but I just can't imagine life without you. I'm so, so, sorry."

I was trying to take in all she'd said when she started to cry again. I took some tissues from the box on the table, wiped my own eyes with one and handed another to her.

"You're not saying anything, Peter. Please, just tell me what you're going to do."

"I was following Sally's advice," I told her, "listening and letting you talk it all out. Damn it, Hannah, you must realise how I've been feeling. It seemed my worst fears about losing you were coming true. I couldn't bear thinking about you with someone else. Now, I'm trying to think of any problems there might be with what you've told me. I'm going to be a dad and I'm going to get married. Try as I can, I can't find anything wrong with the idea. For God's sake, you crazy woman, did you really think I would turn you down?" I held my arms open and felt an overwhelming sense of relief when she walked into them.

*

We decided to stay the night at the bungalow. She told me it belonged to one of her nana's old friends and it had been in their family for years. It was quite primitive – what would be called off-grid nowadays – but at that moment I wouldn't have cared if it had been a shed. In the evening, we drove down to The Kings Inn in Georgeham and managed to get a table. Good pub food, I thought, but a little unimaginative according to Hannah. I really didn't care that much. The stress of the previous few days had taken my appetite away. Now the source of my stress was gone, any food put in front of me would soon disappear.

She told me over dinner that she had missed a period and was a week overdue with a second. She was sure she was pregnant, but would see Dr Marston the following week to get it confirmed. She'd told her nana, which I guess was the reason behind Esmé's phone call to me. It was going well, but I thought she was still a little nervous, and there was something else she needed to tell me.

We got back to the bungalow just as the sun was setting. The view out to sea was to the west. We had the perfect vantage point and watched the sun as it slowly dropped beyond the horizon, turning the sky from blue to a glowing red. We stayed sitting on the bench for a while taking it all in. It was a moment that would stay with me for a long time. I realised it was getting late and we were both exhausted. I didn't want to spoil the evening, so I decided to wait until the morning before trying to discover what else was troubling Hannah.

The curtains were thin and no guard against the strength of the morning sunlight. I managed to slip out of bed without disturbing Hannah, picked up my clothes and headed for the kitchen in search of coffee. The cooker and the fridge were both run on bottled gas, something I hadn't come across before. I filled the kettle and placed it on the hob, then waited for what seemed like ages before the kettle finally began to boil. By then, I could hear Hannah heading towards the bathroom.

We took our coffee to the table by the sitting room window where we had a clear view of Lundy. "West Glyn might have primitive facilities," Hannah told me, "but one would have to search far and wide to find a more stunning location."

After breakfast, we took cups of tea to the bench outside. Hannah pointed to a pair of buzzards soaring in the sky above the valley. Not long after they'd disappeared over the hill, a flock of black-headed gulls began their effortless aerobatics on the warm thermal currents. The day promised to be a hot one, and I was thinking we might go to the beach, but before I mentioned it I needed to know what was on Hannah's mind. I was about to ask when she turned to face me.

"I've been dreading telling you this, but it's happened twice and I don't want to be alone in his company ever again. Peter, it's Seth; the first time he made a pass at me I brushed it off. The second time it wasn't so easy. He had me cornered in the office when I dropped off the plans you'd just completed for the Westbury townhouse. He seemed to be suggesting I should move you out and join forces with him. He was actually walking towards me as if to grab me when he heard the outer office door. It was Joyce. I mumbled something about being in a hurry and rushed past her. I think she knew something had happened. I've been putting off telling you, because, even though he's not a great deal older than you, I know you thought him a friend and a mentor."

I was dumbstruck. Seth knew how devoted I was to Hannah. What was he thinking?

"You've got to believe that I have never given him any sort of encouragement."

"Of course you haven't. I'll drop the van off on site Monday morning and give John a note for Seth. I might do something stupid if I go to the office."

"Would you mind if we stayed here a little longer? We could just relax for a few days away from it all."

"Yes, you're right – we should. It will allow my anger to ebb and give me time to think. I owe Seth nothing now, but he certainly owes me."

"He should have offered you a partnership instead of trying to proposition me. Once we are married, we'll have access to the Trust funds, so we'll have some capital to draw on. You can set up on your own then, hopefully with a decent van that I can stretch my legs in." She said this with a smile, the first smile I'd seen since I'd arrived.

It was hard to believe Seth had done this. I knew he'd always considered himself a bit of a ladies' man, but how the hell had he come to think he could take Hannah away from me? Fuck him. I'd helped build the business and that was the thanks I'd got. I turned to Hannah.

"You know how I feel about you now, don't you, Hannah? Have all your doubts gone?"

"Oh, Peter, I saw your tears yesterday, felt them on your cheeks and tasted the salt in them as they ran down your face when you kissed me. Of course I know, and what stupid traitorous doubts I had are gone. I was a fool – forgive me."

We drove into Woolacombe later that day so that Hannah could ring Esmé and let her know everything had been worked out between us. I made a short call home, assuring everyone all was well and told them that if Seth should ring I'd be in contact later in the week. We kept quiet about our most important news, as we wanted to tell my parents face-to-face. We spent the next few days talking about the future and being as idle as we could. We agreed that our wedding should be as low-key as possible. What innocents we were, for we hadn't taken into account that the irresistible force that was Esmé might have other ideas.

On the morning we were leaving, Hannah said she had one more thing to tell me. I asked what it was. She saw the worried look on my face and replied with a smile, "There is another reason I'm glad you came. Someone has to empty the Elsan closet."

*

John knew straight away that something was wrong. I gave him the letter I'd written to Seth and the keys to the van, but didn't answer his question as to why I was leaving so suddenly. "If you set up on your own, Peter, let me and Cliff know; we'd come and work with you in a flash." I said I would, but that it might be a while.

I went with Hannah to see Dr Marston on the Wednesday. He asked lots of questions then placed his stethoscope on Hannah's abdomen. He thought it most likely that Hannah's intuition was correct, but he would arrange for some tests to make sure.

It was a few days before we received the results. Straight after Dr Marston had telephoned to say the tests were positive, we rushed upstairs. Esmé and Carl were expecting it, but that didn't stop their tears.

The next day, we went to see my parents. We left it until we knew Sally would be home. Once Sally knew, everyone would know. After the upset with me and Hannah, they were expecting something, but they didn't know what. When Mum answered the door, Hannah held her in a fierce hug and whispered something into her ear. She laughed and said she had three daughters, yet it was her youngest, her son, that was going to make her a grandmother. Dad appeared, shook my hand, and accepted a tight hug from Hannah. Sally came rushing down the stairs, saying, "Did I hear right?"

Friday came and we were half expecting what happened. Around six, the bell rang, and I let my sisters and Melissa in. Hannah was preparing food in the kitchen. Melissa told her to stop as we were all going to El Roble. They'd booked a table and there was to be no argument. As we were about to leave, I noticed Esmé and Carl coming down the stairs to join us. It seemed they were all in on it. When we arrived at the restaurant and found Mum and Dad were there, it was clear that the family Hannah had always wanted had become real. Before we were all seated, Sally turned to me and said, "You better get busy, Peter. If your child is the only one, it's going to be the most spoilt child in the world. Three doting aunties and doting parents and grandparents. God help the little thing!"

CHAPTER 16

Joyce came on Tuesday morning with the money I was owed. She asked if Hannah was there and if she would mind talking to her. I went to the basement and asked Hannah. She was curious and agreed. I led Joyce down to face Hannah. It was obvious that she was nervous and needed to get answers to the questions I thought might be haunting her.

"Why, Hannah? Why did this happen?"

"You're asking the wrong person, Joyce," I said. "Go and ask Seth."

"Did he tell you it was me encouraging him?" asked Hannah.

Joyce nodded. I was becoming angry, but Hannah remained calm.

"Joyce, last weekend I proposed to Peter; I'm carrying his child. Why do you suppose I would have done such a thing?"

"I'm sorry, Hannah; I should have known."

"What will you do now?" I asked

"I'm not sure. I guess this is where the rot sets in, trust ends and suspicion starts. Congratulations, you two; I always thought you were right for each other."

When I left Joyce at the door, she asked me to apologise to Hannah for her. Joyce had been a friend and I was going to miss her, but the sadness on her face told me that it would be some time before our friendship could be rekindled. As long as she was with Seth it would be impossible.

Seth never tried to contact me, never tried to explain, and never apologised, so I didn't apologise when, with Hannah's help and agreement, we set up Hawker Roxford Designs and took some of Seth's best clients from him. Soon after we set up, John and Cliff came and asked to work with us. They complained that Seth had become difficult to work for.

Six months later, a for-sale sign went up on the house Seth owned next door. I never found out for certain why Seth needed to sell, but the rumour was that he'd made a big loss on a new development that grounded. We talked about it with Esmé, and Hannah decided she would use some of her newly released capital to put in an anonymous low offer as a cash buyer. Seth must have been desperate, as he accepted the offer the day after Hannah made it. It was Hawker Roxford Designs' first major project and the signature one that clients would see when they wanted to know what we were capable of.

*

The thing about names is that some remain strong in a family, some are the whimsy of parents wanting to be different and some are given out of the desperation of indecision. When our little girl was born, there was no doubt in our minds. She was to be called Esmé. Sally was right: so many people doting on her meant she needed siblings. Hannah, a mother besotted with her firstborn, agreed. Somehow she managed to fit her studies around looking after the two girls and one boy we gave life to. I worked from home as much as possible. It took another three years before Hannah finally gained her doctorate.

POSTSCRIPT

Now, you might ask, what happened to the other people in this story? Well, Jenny took courses in teaching English as a foreign language and moved to Madrid with Melissa, where they eventually set up a language school. They adopted two young orphans from Romania and are now matriarchs presiding over an ever-growing family. Caroline moved to London with Ian, but they broke up because she came to dislike sitting endlessly in bars while Ian was playing. She realised that she was really a home bird and moved back with Mum and Dad until she found Matt, got married and started adding grandchildren to Mum and Dad's roster. Sally and Gareth stayed friends until they finally realised that life without each other would have been unbearable and moved into the basement flat.

I found out later that Craig had been telling the truth about the peregrine falcons on the Crescent. However, it was clear he was obsessed with Hannah, and I think it was this that Tamsin was hinting at when she visited me at the flat. Craig eventually gained a name for himself as a wildlife photographer, but only after moving to York to be near his sister.

Johnny and Tim moved up to London for a while. Tim found it harder to break into the jazz scene than he'd imagined. After a few years, they moved back to Bristol.

Joyce left Seth a few years later when she found out Seth was having an affair with a client. Dougie quit his job with Seth and came to work with us, which opened up a path for us to rebuild our friendship with Joyce. Dougie was full of ideas, so eventually we encouraged him to study design. He became one of our best designers.

After Esmé and Carl passed away, we redesigned the house, but the basement remained more or less how it was when Hannah and I had lived there. Over the years, it has been a refuge for many family members and the current resident is one of our eldest granddaughters, a bright young girl called Petra who is studying at university.

So what about Hannah and me? At this moment, Hannah is reading the younger grandchildren stories in the playroom she designed for visiting young ones. It seems that, against all the odds, we made it.

The End

Printed in Dunstable, United Kingdom